Sherlock's Secretary

By Chris Chan

Paperback ISBN 978-1-78705-884-2
ePub ISBN 978-1-78705-885-9
PDF ISBN 978-1-78705-886-6

Published by MX Publishing
335 Princess Park Manor, Royal Drive,
London, N11 3GX
www.mxpublishing.com

Cover design by Brian Belanger

This book is dedicated to my parents, Drs. Carlyle and Patricia Chan.
And to Steve Emecz, Brian Belanger, Derrick Belanger, and David Marcum for their encouragement and like-minded enthusiasm for all things Sherlock Holmes-related.

Contents

CHAPTER ONE
The Bank Robbery

Inspector Dankworth was looking at me as if I were completely insane, and I can't say that I blamed him. "No, you're not," he told me with firm conviction.

"Sir, I can assure you that I am." I didn't blame him for his skepticism, but he was wrong and I was right.

"Mr. Zhuang, Sherlock Holmes is a fictional character. You can't be his secretary."

"Well, the Baker Street Irregulars might disagree with the first part of what you just said..." My voice trailed off as I realized that the man sitting across from me was not in the mood to hear about the more complex points of Sherlockian scholarship. "I think there's a bit of confusion here. I'm not actually Sherlock Holmes' secretary. That's just my job title."

A faint flicker passed over the inspector's face, and he appeared to be willing to consider the possibility that I was not totally bonkers. "You mean you work as a personal assistant for one of those actors who plays Sherlock Holmes on the telly?"

"No, nothing like that. You see, the bank where I work is located on Baker Street."

"Isn't that where Sherlock Holmes lived?"

"Yes, before he retired and moved–" I stopped myself. The inspector wasn't the sort of man who would appreciate a digression. "It's a big building, and one of the street numbers that bank sits on is technically 221B Baker Street. Well, you'd be amazed how many people all over the world send letters addressed to "Mr. Sherlock Holmes at 221B Baker Street." Sacks of them every week."

The inspector's jaw dropped, making all three of his chins jiggle. "What's wrong with those people? Don't they know they're sending letters to a man who doesn't exist?"

"Well, they believe in him, and the postmen keep delivering the letters to the bank. It's a bit like *Miracle on 34th Street*."

"I thought you said this was on Baker Street."

This threw me for a second. "I'm talking about the classic Christmas film..." The inspector obviously hadn't seen it, so I moved on with my narrative. "Well for many years now, the bank has decided that it's a clever public relations move to have somebody answering all those letters. Some people want an autograph from Mr. Holmes, and other people have a problem they want him to solve. That's where I come in. I write responses to all of those letters. I've got reams and reams of special stationary with a special letterhead on it, saying, "From the desk of Mr. Sherlock Holmes." If there's a serious problem, I refer them to the proper authorities. If somebody just wants to know what Holmes and Doctor Watson have been up to lately, I give them a brief account of their latest case, usually an original story I wrote. It seems to make a lot of people happy. I get so many thank you notes. It's very gratifying."

The inspector's eyes looked as if they were about to pop out of his head. "Hell. And you get paid for this?"

"Oh, yes. Not a lot, mind you, but my salary covers my expenses, and my needs are pretty modest. Of course, in the future–"

"And I thought my dotty sister-in-law had a racket for a job. She's got a tiny room in the back of a vegan restaurant where she waves her hands over silly people and fixes their auras or something like that."

"Are her customers satisfied?"

3

"Well, they can't very well take her into court and prove that there hasn't been any improvement to their auras, can they?" The inspector pulled out a grubby handkerchief and dabbed the perspiration off his brow. "Do you know how my seventeen-year-old daughter plans to make a living?

"No idea, sir."

"She wants to be a TikToker. She wants to post short videos on the Internet featuring her making a fool of herself and get paid for it."

"I was not aware that was a thing."

"Nor was I. When I was growing up, we had this wild notion that you actually had to *work* in order to make a living." Inspector Dankworth ran his hand over his face. "Mr. Zhuang…"

"Please, call me Addy."

"Addy?"

"Short for Adalbert."

"Adalbert Zhuang? Where'd you get a name like that?"

"My mother's family fled to England from Poland when they were being threatened for their involvement in Solidarity, and my father's family emigrated from Hong Kong not long after the British announced the upcoming transfer of power."

4

"Ah. Well, Addy, I've been having a migraine coming on all day, and I'd say it's about five minutes away from making an appearance. What say you give me a summary of what happened to you this afternoon in the fewest possible words, please?

"Of course. You see, I'd come back from a late lunch about an hour earlier, and the day's post had been delivered to my office. Do you need to know what I had for lunch?"

"I do not."

"Right. Well, it was a surprisingly large delivery that day, over forty envelopes. So, I hung up my coat and sat down at my desk and started opening and sorting the letters. I was nearly done when two men burst into my office without knocking. One shut the door, and before I could ask what they were doing, one of them pulled a gigantic knife out of his coat and put a finger over his mouth."

"Can you describe them?"

"Yes. Both were around six feet tall, maybe a little under. One had a long brown coat and a matching hat, and the other had a long grey coat with a black hat. Stocky builds, but that might have been padding. Both wore thick glasses and had large noses and substantial beards. I'm pretty sure the beards and noses were fake, and the glasses probably didn't have prescription lenses, but I didn't get a good look at them, because before I knew it, one of them put the knife to my throat, and the other was pulling my hands behind my back and binding them together with zip ties, and then they trussed up my feet as well and put a bit of tape over my mouth. Then they took the belt from my dressing-gown–"

"Dressing-gown? You have a dressing gown at the office?"

"Oh, yes. You see, several times a week, the bank takes visitors around, and they all want to see my office. When I first started, it was just a plain, ordinary office, and people on the tour were disappointed. So, the bank gave me a nice little budget, and I did a lot of decorating. There's a bunch of bookcases filled with copies of the original stories and new adventures by modern authors and scholarly works on Sherlock Holmes. There are some framed posters of the original Sidney Paget illustrations on the walls, and pictures of the actors in costume, and stills from the films and TV shows up on the walls, too. And I've got all sorts of memorabilia I found cheap on eBay, like a plaster bust of Holmes, and a rack of meerschaum pipes, even though I don't smoke, and a violin– not a Stradivarius but a nice instrument, a set of nesting dolls with the characters, and a chess set with the characters as playing pieces, and so many other statuettes and knickknacks and commemorative plates and other things. In the corner, on the coat hooks, I have one for my own coat, and then there's an Inverness cape and deerstalker hat on one hook, and a Cumberbatch wool cape coat on another, and a dressing-gown like Holmes wears on the last hook. So that's where the belt came from, and they used it to secure me to my chair."

"I see."

"I used to wear it sometimes when I was working, but one of my supervisors said this was a place of business, not the Playboy Mansion, so I stopped."

"Very sensible."

"They don't have a problem with my wearing the Inverness or the cape coat around the bank, though."

From the little vein I could see throbbing in his brow, Inspector Dankworth's migraine was just about to announce its triumphant arrival, but he soldiered on and continued the interview. "So, you were all tied up…"

"That's right. They wheeled my chair around so I was facing the wall, and I was just thinking I should say a few prayers and get my soul right with God, when I heard one of them say– by the way, they were clearly pitching their voices a couple of octaves lower than they naturally were– "Here it is! Let's get out of here!" Then the next thing you know, they're out the door, and I'm sitting there, trying to get loose or make a bit of noise. A couple of hours later, when I was wishing that I'd used the restroom before heading back to work, the charwoman walked into my office to start the evening cleaning, found me, cut me loose, and after taking care of a pressing matter, I called you."

The Inspector took a sip from his mug, clearly wishing it was something stronger. "What did they take?"

"The three envelopes in the "Non-Criminal Investigations" pile."

After a long, deep breath, the Inspector groaned, "I know I'm going to regret asking this, but how many piles are there?"

"There are seven piles. The first is the 'Holmes fans' pile, who want to know what the detective's up to now, or who want an autograph or something. I'm happy to oblige. It's fun to write a couple of little paragraphs about the latest case, or linking Holmes to recent events. And I'm authorized, so it's not forgery to sign Holmes' name."

"Wouldn't Holmes be a hundred and fifty years old by now?"

"Give or take a bit, depending on who's estimating his birth date. If you go by Baring-Gould–" One glance at the Inspector's eyes told me that he was in no mood to hear about the Sherlockian scholarship of William S. Baring-Gould. "The people writing don't care. The second pile is for people with questions about the Holmes' stories. Most of those questions I know off the top of my head, sometimes I need to do a bit of research. The third pile is for fans of the actors in various adaptations, like Robert Downey Jr. or Benedict Cumberbatch or Jonny Lee Miller. I send those on to their various agents and publicists. Pile four is for letters addressed to Basil of Baker Street. As he's a licensed Disney character, I'm not permitted to even open those. I have to send those directly to the Disney offices. I was warned very sternly to be careful with those letters, as the copyright lawyers can be more ferocious than the Hound of the Baskervilles. They've always been lovely to me, but I've been following the rules."

"I'm sure you do," the Inspector replied, rubbing his temples.

"Pile five is the one for crank letters or threats–"

"Threats?"

"Uh-huh. People claiming to be Professor Moriarty or Colonel Sebastian Moran or something like that often send threatening letters to Holmes. Other people write angry missives decrying me for being an imposter. Those letters go straight in the recycling bin. The sixth pile is actual crimes. You'd be amazed by how many people want Holmes to track down a missing person or to report abuse to him, or perhaps they claim to have knowledge of a crime. I send those on to Scotland Yard."

"As well you should."

"Uh-huh. The final pile, number seven, is for letters that aren't about actual crimes. That's the Non-Criminal Investigations pile. Sometimes they're letters asking Holmes to investigate a potentially adulterous spouse. I write back to tell them he doesn't do divorce work. Other times children ask Holmes to help him find missing toys. I usually tell them to clean their rooms or retrace their steps, and often a week later I get another letter thanking me when they find their lost teddy bear underneath the couch or something like that. Sometimes people want help battling addiction, and they think that Holmes can assist them because of his kicking his use of cocaine. I refer them to some useful support groups and doctors. You know, stuff like that."

"And it was pile seven that got stolen? Three letters, you said?"

"Yes. I read all three letters, though not too thoroughly, and I can't see why anybody would want to steal them. They were utterly innocuous. Nothing interesting about them. The first was from a woman who wanted Holmes to investigate her fiancé, whom she thought was cheating on her. The second was from a man who wanted Holmes to help him find a lost item. The letter didn't specify what it was. The third letter was odd. It wanted Holmes to help track down a long-lost Sherlock Holmes television movie.

That's all I can remember. I usually skim the letters once and then read them more carefully later."

"That's it? Just those three?"

"Yes."

"No other letters were taken? None of the knickknacks or anything else were stolen?"

"Absolutely nothing else, Inspector. They didn't touch my wallet, and my watch is still on my wrist."

"They didn't... hurt you in any way, did they?"

"No. They didn't even leave a bruise. It wasn't very comfortable being trussed up in that chair, but I'm fine now."

"So, when it comes down to it, all they did was steal three pieces of junk mail?"

I don't like to think of what's sent to me as junk mail, but I nodded.

The Inspector leaned back in his chair. "We'll look into this of course, but I hope you understand that this can't be our highest priority. If they'd taken a million pounds or something, or if someone wound up dead, we'd put our best people on this. But I see dozens of people getting robbed and beaten far worse than you were every week, and quite frankly, Addy, you got off easy."

"Oh yes, Inspector, I agree. I always know to count my blessings."

"You know what I think happened?"

"Please tell me, sir."

"I think that you were the victim of a prank. Some university students trying to get into a fraternity. There are some groups that require pledges to steal something from a Member of Parliament or a bank. I think that's what happened. They set out to take something distinctive but worthless from a bank in order to be admitted into some silly group, and you were just in the wrong place at the wrong time."

"Oh."

The inspector arched an eyebrow. "Don't you agree with me?"

"Well yes, sir. That makes perfect sense. I've been trying to figure out why someone took those letters, and your idea seems to explain it. Why else would anyone do that?"

"Exactly. I'll do my due diligence, never fear, but I'm nearly positive that this is all just a pointless prank." He nodded firmly, assuring himself of the wisdom of his own conclusions. "How did you get that job, anyway?"

"Well you see, two years ago I attended a meeting of a Sherlock Holmes Society, and I overheard the manager of the bank saying how they were looking for someone to work for them as the "secretary" to Sherlock Holmes. The person who used to fill the role retired and moved to Portugal. He wanted someone with a background in mystery writing, as they needed a person who could write a lot of original flash fiction about Holmes' most recent adventures for anybody who asked about what he's up to now. And I want to be a mystery writer, sir. I studied creative writing at university—"

"Money well spent, eh?"

I put up with a lot of comments like that. I've learned to ignore them. "And I've written quite a bit. Seven novels, three plays, and twenty-eight short stories."

"Have they all been published?"

"Er, no. Only two of the short stories have been published in some little magazines."

"How little are these magazines?"

"They both folded not long after my stories were printed. Anyway, I introduced myself to the bank manager, he told me to stop by for an interview, and I dropped by the next day and hammered out responses to three letters and was hired on the spot. As I said, it's a good job, sir. Decent pay. Not spectacular, but it covers my bills and allows me to put a bit into savings. It's fun work, and if I finish my replies, I can do research consisting of reading Sherlock Holmes books or watching DVD's of Sherlock Holmes adaptations. And if I want, I can use my extra time to work on my own writing. I'm nearly done with my eighth novel."

"Eighth? Think this'll be the one that finally gets published?"

"I can only hope so, sir."

"Well, good luck to you." The inspector waved a hand towards the door. "I'll let you know if there are any developments, but don't hold your breath."

"Thank you, sir. I shan't, sir."

The grunt the inspector made in reply seemed almost friendly to me, and when he waved his hand towards the door, I wished him well and made my way out of the building. As I wandered through the halls, I wondered if the events of the afternoon had really happened. Might this all be some sort of bizarre daydream after my lunch hadn't settled comfortably on my stomach? After feeling the force from a rather strongly built officer colliding with me, I was assured that I was not, in fact, the victim of my own subconscious.

I was just wondering about how I was going to get home when I noticed my best friend and flatmate Sanna Mahabir leaning against the wall. Sanna and I first met at university. By rights, we shouldn't have gotten along. We have almost nothing in common. Our views on politics, religion, economics, entertainment, food, and fashion are almost entirely diametrically opposed. And yet... we get along splendidly. We really get and accept each other, and it's pretty hard to find someone like that. After university, Sanna discovered a terrific flat she couldn't afford, so we decided to join forces with a third friend of ours from university– whom I'll introduce later.

"Did they give you the third degree, Addy?"

I managed a smile at her question. "Not really. It was all very pleasant."

"Come on. You can tell me everything that happened over dinner."

As we headed out the door, I thought to turn my mobile phone back on, and discovered there was a message from the bank manager. Asking for Sanna's indulgence, I called him back, and after four rings I heard a familiar gravelly voice.

"Ah, Addy. How'd the interrogation go?"

"Quite well, thanks."

"And you're feeling fine?"

"Absolutely, sir. Tip-top condition, thank you for asking."

"Excellent, excellent. Listen, Addy, the reason I called is because I don't want you to feel like you have to come in to work tomorrow."

"I'm appreciate the thought sir, but I'm perfectly all right."

"Of course you are, but these things can be traumatic. Why don't you take a full week off with full pay, and I'll see you in seven days?"

I was about to argue further, but Sanna, who apparently could hear the conversation, nudged me none too gently in the ribs. "Take the free vacation!" she hissed.

A moment's thought led me to see the justice in this perspective, and I ceased my resistance and accepted my employer's kind offer. A few minutes later, Sanna and I were comfortably ensconced in a booth at a gastropub she's very fond of (though I find it overpriced and pretentious), and placed our orders.

"So," Sanna folded her hands in front of her and leaned forward. "Tell me everything."

I took a breath and repeated the story of my experiences to her. It didn't take very long, and I finished just as the server brought us our meal.

Satisfied that she was fully caught up with my experiences, Sanna slid her spoon into a crimson stew on top of a bed of rice. I was just thinking that my chicken sandwich would have been a lot more enjoyable without the bizarre aioli they liberally spread upon it, but I was too hungry to complain.

"Is there a problem with the chicken?"

"Why would you ask that?"

"The look on your face. You look like your sandwich has gotten drunk and belligerent and has insulted your mother."

"It's the aioli. I have no idea what it's trying to be, but it's failing."

Sanna picked up her spoon and scraped off a little bit of the aioli. Tasting it, she pronounced, "It's harissa-lavender."

"Seriously? Who in their right minds would decide that those two flavors should be combined, let alone spread on chicken?"

"Not everybody believes that bottled ketchup, mustard, and brown sauce are the only acceptable condiments, Zhuang. Are you going to make that face for the rest of the meal?"

"No, the chips are quite decent."

"Very well, Mr. Adventurous Eater. What do you think you'll do with your week off?"

I hadn't thought about that until she asked. I had neither the funds nor the inclination to travel anywhere. I figured that I should spend a bit of time with my family, but I wanted to put off telling my mother about the bank robbery for as long as possible, worrying that as soon as she heard about what had just happened to me, she'd freak out and insist that I work from home in the future for my own safety. When I expressed my concerns to Sanna, she agreed.

"I'm not saying you should keep the robbery from your mother," she explained, "I'm just suggesting you find a more convenient time to tell her, preferably in the distant future, such as in a few more decades when age-related hearing loss sets in and you can tell her without her actually understanding what you're saying."

"I doubt that's a viable plan, Sanna."

"Well, you never know until you try, do you?" She took a long sip of her lemon squash. "Do you think they'll ever catch the people who robbed you? I don't believe they'll even look for them. Stealing a few letters from people who think that Sherlock Holmes is real isn't high on their list of priorities."

"Probably not. I mean, I don't blame them. Why bother with this case when there are actual murders to solve?"

"But why would they steal those letters in the first place?"

I reminded her of the inspector's fraternity initiation theory. "Maybe..." Sanna said, unconvinced. "But I can't shake the sense that there was a really important reason for the heist."

"But the letters were worthless."

"Maybe they were..." Sanna snapped her fingers. "What about the stamps? Suppose there's some wealthy old philatelist with dementia, and now he believes that Sherlock Holmes is alive and well and happy to look into a case for him. Then he sticks one of his rarest and most valuable stamps on the envelope and mails it. When his children or his caretaker come to visit him, they're horrified to see the gap in his stamp album, and they question him, and he tells them he wrote a letter to Sherlock Holmes. Well, they know that the guy's senility has just cost them fifty thousand pounds, or however much the stamp is worth. They don't want to call you and ask for the envelope back, because they're afraid that you'll pocket the stamp yourself. So they burst in, take the envelope back, and there you are!"

Sanna looked so triumphant at her own brilliance that I hated to burst her bubble. "Why did they take all three envelopes?"

"As a decoy, to keep from drawing attention from the one letter they were really interested in!"

I supposed that was possible. "I always look at the stamps, just to see what people are using. I don't recall seeing any old or unusual-looking stamps. Just ordinary self-sticking ones."

"It doesn't have to be an old stamp. Maybe it's a more recent stamp, but due to an engraver's error it looks like the Queen has a moustache or something like that."

"I didn't notice anything like that..."

My eyes rolled upwards as my voice trailed off, and Sanna waited patiently for about three seconds before asking me just what the heck was going on in my mind.

"I was just remembering that there's a chance that I have a picture of those stamps," I explained. "Today, this one young woman from Hoboken, New Jersey, sent me this beautiful piece of fan art of some of the actors who played Holmes. It's really nice. I'm hoping that the bank will give me the money to buy a nice, cheap frame for it and hang it on the wall. I wanted to show it to you, so I took a picture so I didn't have to carry the poster with me." As I pulled out my mobile," I continued explaining, saying "I spread out the poster on my desk and weighted it down, but the "Non-Criminal Investigations" pile was on the right, and I think that they're in the picture."

Handing my mobile to Sanna, I told her, "Take a look. That's some pretty impressive artistry, isn't it? It looks just like the actors."

"Yeah, terrific." Sanna swiped the screen. "You're right. The "Non-Criminal Investigations" pile is there. And the three envelopes are spread out, so all the stamps are visible… but you can't zoom in far enough to really scrutinize them. If there's a subtle flaw in the stamps, I can't see it. But you're right. At first glance, they just look like ordinary, current stamps."

"I guess there's no way to confirm your theory, then."

Sanna pushed my mobile back to me. "Well, until I see actual evidence proving otherwise, I'm going to assume I'm right about a rare and valuable stamp."

We talked a little more, but we made no more progress in figuring out the motives for the robbery. After finishing our meal, we made our way home, changing buses twice and walking as fast as we could to beat an approaching rainstorm. We made it to the flat just as the droplets started falling, and as we made our way inside, we noticed that the red light was on outside of our flatmate Jasper's bedroom. We're used to that, as Jasper is a professional YouTuber who makes his living through monetized videos. When the light's on, he's recording, so we have to be a bit cautious with our noise levels, even though he's done a pretty fair job in soundproofing his room. I'd thought of telling Inspector Dankworth about Jasper's success, as a means of reassuring him that his daughter's TikTok career wasn't as harebrained as he seemed to think, but I'd held my tongue as soon as I realized that Dankworth wouldn't have appreciated this bit of information.

"So, now that you've had some time to think about it, do you have any plans for your vacation?" Sanna asked.

"I just want to take it easy. Read a few books, work on my new novel, send out some more query letters to agents. Maybe catch up on some more Zabel Carvalho podcasts and videos."

"She's the one you fancy, right?"

"I don't!"

"Sure you do. I've seen the longing look on your face when you watch her mini-documentaries. I don't blame you. She's very pretty. Great hair, the kind of smile you see in your dreams…"

"She's a very good true crime reporter."

"Oh, she's talented. And totally lush."

"All right, enough."

Sanna giggled. "When was the last time you had a proper date with an actual woman? Was it when we were in university?"

"Yes. You should know. You set me up with that mental case."

"On paper, I thought she'd be a good match for you. You love classic mysteries, she said she loved *Midsomer Murders*… How was I to know she'd been arrested for stalking Neil Dudgeon?"

"I'm not blaming you, I'm just saying the date was rather… traumatic."

"Well, chalk it up to experience, mate. Get some sleep, and when you wake up, try to think of something original and fun to do with your holiday."

I showered and reread a few chapters in an Anthony Berkeley book for the tenth time, before dozing off rather earlier than I normally do, around ten. I guess the adrenaline I'd gotten from being robbed wore off, and I crashed.

At seven, I was awakened by the sound of someone knocking at the entry door to our apartment. As I stumbled out of my room, I heard Sanna calling out from the kitchen, "Can you get that? I'm going to be late for work!"

I peered through the peephole and did a double take. As I pulled open the door, I expected to see that I'd been imagining the person on the other side, but wonder of wonders, my eyes actually weren't deceiving me. The most beautiful woman I'd ever seen in my life was smiling at me.

"Hello! Are you Adalbert Zhuang?"

My tongue was tied into a sheepshank knot, so I just nodded mutely.

"I'm Zabel Carvalho, the true crime reporter. I'd like to interview you about yesterday's robbery."

CHAPTER TWO
Breakfast and Theorizing

I gulped a few times, trying to choose my words carefully. I had the odd sensation that if I were to speak, my voice would be an octave or two higher than desirable, so I attempted to deepen my tone. Before I could say a word, however, Jasper came sprinting out of his room.

"Is that my breakfast pizza? That was quick!" Jasper rushed up to the door with a hand full of money. "You're a lot prettier than the regular pizza guy."

"She's not delivering your pizza!" I didn't mean to shout. It just slipped out without my meaning to alter my usual tone.

"Pizza for breakfast again, Jasper? Would it kill you to have porridge or yoghurt one of these mornings?" Sanna wandered out of the kitchen with a carton of strawberry yoghurt in one hand. "It's good for you."

"Breakfast pizza is a proper meal. It has sausage, bacon, tomatoes, scrambled eggs, mushrooms... It's a full breakfast only the toast is on the bottom and there's cheese on it, which actually makes it better than a standard breakfast."

Sanna probably would have replied with a cutting remark about his cholesterol, but she recognized Zabel and was nearly as dumbstruck as I was. "Have I wandered in on one of your dreams, Addy?" she finally asked.

Zabel laughed. "I can assure you this is really happening."

As Jasper slunk over to the side of the room, disappointed that his pizza hadn't arrived, Sanna looked at me, and when she realized that my vocal cords weren't in working order, she kindly took control of the situation. "Won't you come on in?"

Zabel flashed a dazzling smile, and Sanna gestured towards the most comfortable chair. "Can I take your coat?" I asked a moment too late. She'd already sat down.

"Thanks, but I was hoping to leave in a minute to take you to breakfast."

"Breakfast?"

"Yes. You haven't eaten yet, have you?"

"No, I haven't!" Suddenly, I realized that I was ferociously hungry. "Where would you like to go?"

"There's a café down the street. The owners are friends of mine. If you'd be willing to talk about your experiences while we eat, that'd be lovely. Then maybe you could come over to my recording studio."

Before I could respond with a jubilant "Definitely!" Jasper scowled and grumbled, "When the real pizza delivery person comes, let me know." With that, he clomped back to his room.

A bit later than I'd planned, I told Zabel "Definitely! Are you ready to go?"

She gave me a look that showed that she was starting to question how sound my mind was. "Wouldn't you like to get dressed first?"

Looking down and realizing I was still in my pajamas, I responded, "Right. Would you mind waiting five minutes, please?" Before I could shut the door to my room, Sanna squeezed in behind me.

"Don't mess this up, Addy."

"I beg your pardon?"

"I know that you're genetically predisposed to find it nearly impossible to play it cool, but do yourself a favor and remember to take a deep breath every once and a while around this woman. I know it's hard to believe– certainly I was blindsided by it– but you might actually have a chance with her."

"Are you sure?"

"Women know women, Addy. You were too busy hyperventilating to notice, but I caught her looking you up and down and trying to repress a smile of appreciation. Yeah, she's an eleven out of ten, but if you actually paid a bit of attention to your clothes and your hair, in the right light, you could be a solid eight."

"Is that supposed to be a complement?"

"It's a warning. Don't mess this up. This is the first great chance you've had since that fashion model at university lost her contact lenses and you gallantly led her back to her flat."

"It wasn't my fault that when we got there, her boyfriend– and her other boyfriend– were fighting right in front of the door."

"At least the black eye you got made you look rugged. Now, shave and fix your hair, and make sure not to mix up your razor and your comb. Brush your teeth and gargle mouthwash, and when you come out, put on the clothes I lay out for you. I know what she'll like. Now go!"

I did as I was told, and as I looked at myself in the mirror wearing the dress shirt, grey trousers, and navy-blue jumper Sanna selected for me, I was fairly certain she'd made wise choices.

Inflating and deflating my lungs, I tried to walk out of my room as casually as possible. "You look very nice," Zabel told me, with Sanna flashing me a thumbs-up behind her.

"Thanks," I said, taking my coat off the hanger. As I held the door open for her, Zabel nearly careened into a man who filled the entire doorway.

"I've got a breakfast pizza here for–"

Zabel and I nudged him to one side and hurried out to avoid being knocked down by Jasper's race for the door, and five minutes later I found myself in a corner table with gigantic frosted windows on both sides and enough curly ferns surrounding us to qualify as a rainforest.

"It's nice and private here," Zabel beamed at me.

I was temporarily rendered mute when I caught the prices on the menu. Zabel may have read my face when she assured me, "This is on me, of course."

Apprehensive about ordering the wrong thing– one of my last dates was over before it even began when the lady accompanying me to breakfast informed me that she could never be with a man who ate kippers– I asked her, "What do you recommend?"

"Try the salmon with scrambled eggs, and get the homemade crumpets. They make the jams themselves."

"That sounds nice." The waitress seemed to approve of my order, and Zabel asked for the poached eggs with avocado and tomatoes.

"And when you bring the coffee, leave the full pot, please."

"Yes, ma'am. I remember."

Zabel shrugged. "I'm a regular here. So. Let's get right to it. Tell me everything that happened to you yesterday. Leave out nothing."

I complied, and moments after I'd wrapped up my story, our meals arrived. After thanking the waitress, Zabel closed her eyes for a few seconds and her lips twitched. I couldn't tell if she was trying to appreciate the smell of the food or saying a quick grace, but partly out of genuine gratitude for the food and partly to stay on her good side, I made sure she saw my head was bowed too when her eyes opened.

The food was indeed quite appetizing, but it tasted expensive, as if pound notes had been shredded and mixed into the eggs. The bright orange color from the yolks indicated that these were the kind of specialty farm-raised eggs from chickens given more care and attention than Prince William and Duchess Kate's kids, and there were unidentifiable herbs sprinkled on top of the salmon that indicated that the cook was too pretentious to fob ordinary parsley off on the customers.

"Do you like it?"

I nodded. "Thanks for the recommendation. It's very good. Much better than my usual breakfast fare."

"What do you normally have?"

"Cold cereal. Nothing special, but it fits my budget."

Zabel's smile wasn't easy to decipher. "Is that a criticism of my spending too much money on lavish meals?"

"What? No! I wasn't criticizing you at all!"

"I'm not rich, you know."

"Well, you are wearing designer clothes, your hair looks like it was done by a top stylist, and that watch is Cartier."

For a second, it looked as if she were about to grab her orange juice glass and throw it in my face, but luckily for me, she burst out laughing. "Oh, my God. You're doing the Sherlock Holmes thing. You're scrutinizing me and trying to figure out stuff about me by observing the little details. Have you spent so much time studying Sherlock Holmes that you think you can tell what I'm like?"

There was no point in trying to deny it. "Do you mind?"

"Not at all. I've tried to develop the same skills myself. I saw you checking out my left hand earlier and observing that I don't wear a ring, but I thought that was just normal guy reconnaissance on a new woman he met." She set down her fork and leaned back. "Well, go on. What do you think you know about me? And no fair repeating things you read on my website or Wikipedia page."

I hesitated. "All right. Well, from the absence of a smell and the lack of stains on your fingers and teeth, I'm saying non-smoker."

"Right."

"You live in a house with a garage, not a flat."

Her eyes narrowed a bit. "Correct. How'd you know?"

"When we rode down here in your car, I saw the garage door opener clipped to the sun visor. But you just made a big point of saying that you're not rich, so I guess you didn't buy it yourself. You could live with at least one housemate, but I noticed the hospital parking lot slips on your dashboard. Four of them. You look like you're in good health to me, so I'm wondering if you live with someone with serious health problems. A parent or a grandparent, maybe?"

I couldn't tell if I was seeing a glint of respect or annoyance in her eyes. "My aunt has breast cancer. We're very close, and I moved in with her six months ago to care for her."

"That's nice of you. Also, I think you play football for fun. And you played on Saturday afternoon."

It was at this point that Zabel started to appear a little alarmed. "Have you been stalking me?"

"No! It's the Sherlock Holmes observation thing, like I told you!"

"O.K. Tell me how you figured it out and I'll apologize for accusing you of stalking." She glanced down at her purse. "I know you could've guessed that I'm a football fan from the charm on my car keys."

"Yes. I noticed a little clump of dried mud on the floor on the driver's side of the car. It had holes on it, clearly it–"

"–Was from a football cleat," Zabel finished.

"I saw the charm on your keys, that's why I thought it was football and not rugby. If you had mud in your cleat, it would have to had rained, but not too long ago, or it would've crumbled. The most recent time it rained was after dark last night, and you didn't have time to play this morning. The last time before that when it rained was Saturday morning– it poured for three hours and stopped around lunch. So you could've played in the afternoon or evening…"

"Got it." Zabel laughed. "You know, watching the adaptations of Sherlock Holmes, I never got why some people were so upset when Holmes was able to figure out so much stuff about people just by looking at them. Now I understand the dual feelings of first thinking 'There's no way he could know that!' followed immediately afterwards by, 'Oh. That makes sense.'" She laughed. "I apologize for suspecting you of stalking."

"Quite all right."

"By the way, regarding my clothes and watch? I know a film and television production company that sells costumes and whatnot after they're done. Pretty steep markdown. One of my sisters is a skilled stylist, so she does my hair free. And as for this restaurant–" she waved her hand. "The owners of this place have a son who was wrongly accused of breaking and entering. I was digging up some CCTV for a piece on a different case I was doing, I wound up proving their son's alibi. So now I get free breakfasts. No complementary lunches or dinners, though. I think that'd cut into their profits a little too deeply."

"That's brilliant. How many cases have you solved since you started covering true crime cases?"

Zabel looked a bit embarrassed. "Well, I've never actually solved a case. I mean, I was able to prove the kid I just mentioned innocent, but I didn't figure out who really committed the robbery. And I've never identified a person who's guilty of something or gotten a wrongly convicted person out of prison. I just make videos and write articles about crimes that other people solved, or sometimes I cover crimes that weren't solved at all. My videos get pretty decent traffic, so the advertising revenue covers my expenses. I studied journalism at university, but when I couldn't find a decent job after graduation I followed my interests in true crime and went into business for myself. I wrote a few pieces for some lurid websites and led some Jack the Ripper night tours before I finally started making my own little crime documentary videos. So, enough about me, Sherlock's secretary. How about you? How'd you get your job?"

I told her my employment story using pretty much the same words that I used with the inspector the previous day, and she seemed to find the story amusing. "What do your parents think about your job?" Zabel asked.

"They're actually quietly enthusiastic. Mum and Dad are both Sir Arthur Conan Doyle fans, and Mum's always loved the idea of my being a writer. She's a literature professor, by the way. I just need to get my books published. And Dad wanted at least one of his children to follow in his footsteps, but maybe one of my younger sisters will, as my older brother has let Dad down."

"What does your father do?"

"He's a doctor. When he and my mother met, he was fresh out of medical school, and he told her that he had excellent prospects, predicting that in ten

38

years he'd be one of the most respected proctologists in London. And he was right."

"And that line won over your mother?"

"Well, he didn't exactly sweep her off her feet right away, but the more she got to know him, the better she liked him, and finally she said she'd be delighted to marry him if he promised not to bring his work home with him."

"What does your older brother do? It sounds like he decided against being a doctor."

"Oh, no. He went to medical school, but he decided to specialize in ear, nose, and throat; which when you think about it is nearly as far as you can get from proctology, anatomically speaking. As far as I know, Dad's never come out and said anything to my brother, but there's a little bit of tension."

Zabel shrugged. "Well, we've all got to follow our own paths." After a pause, she scooped up her last bite of avocado-covered eggs and chewed it with a thoughtful expression. Not wanting to interrupt her enjoyment of her final morsel, I remained silent. "Is there anything else about yesterday you didn't mention yet?"

"Not that I can— wait a minute." I pulled out my mobile and pulled up the picture of the artwork, explaining how Sanna had suggested the robbery was all about the stamps, but that they looked perfectly ordinary but a bit blurry in the picture.

"Half a moment…" Zabel started squinting.

"What?"

"The return addresses on the envelopes."

I hadn't really thought about that. "I told you I read their letters. There wasn't anything particularly interesting or notable in them."

"Are you sure? Maybe there was something incriminating in one of the notes?"

"It's not like one of them confessed to plotting to steal the Crown Jewels. Just a trio of letters to Sherlock Holmes, asking him to solve the cases of a possibly cheating fiancé, an unspecified missing item, and a lost movie."

"Well of all those, the cheating fiancé is the most likely. What if he really was cheating, and he got caught and they argued, and he wound up killing her? And maybe before she died, she mentioned she sent a letter to you, and he was afraid that it might give the police a motive, so he was determined to steal the letter back."

I liked her theory a lot. It was imaginative, and I would have really wanted it to be true, had its veracity not meant that a woman had been murdered. But there was another flaw. "Wouldn't stealing the letter be a bit unnecessary? I mean, if he killed her, the police would focus on him immediately. That's standard procedure. If a woman's killed, it's almost always the husband or the fiancé or the boyfriend."

"True enough. In eighty percent of the crimes I've covered about murdered women who were in romantic relationships, their partners were responsible for the deaths. Of course, there were a few attacks by random strangers, a homicidal sister-in-law, and the husbands' mistresses were behind some crimes, too... But you're right. Why risk stealing the letter when the second question the police would ask him, right after 'Did you do it?' is 'Were you cheating?' Why bother stealing the letter when a little digging on the part of the police would uncover credit card charges to seedy hotels and purchases of silky lingerie that weren't in the dead fiancée's size?"

My imagination was running wild, and not just because of the way that Zabel had said the words "silky lingerie." "Maybe there was something incriminating scribbled on the back of one of the letters. Or something invisible, like fingerprints. Or maybe impressions carved onto the paper by someone writing on the piece of paper directly on top of it on the pad. But why would anybody think I'd check for any of those things?"

Zabel tapped her fingers on my mobile. "Remember, these people may not have thought they were writing to you. They thought they were writing to Sherlock Holmes. Maybe they thought he could deduce things about them from clues on the letter. Maybe they worried he'd notice a trace of white powder at the bottom of the letter and deduce that they were heroin smugglers. Or a trace of rare cigarette ash that indicates that they were spies from a foreign power. Yes, I'm aware of how stupid that sounds. I'm brainstorming here, but I don't think lightning is striking anywhere." She sighed. "Do you mind that I emailed the picture to myself? I should've asked first. I'm sorry about that. I was just getting excited and I overreached."

"Please, don't worry about it."

"Thanks." She returned the phone to me and pulled an electronic tablet out of her voluminous purse. "I can get a better look at the photo on this." She ran her fingers over the screen a bit. "And... we have some joy here!" She pulled out a notebook and started scribbling. "The first letter was from a Lacina Berrycloth. The full address is readable, she lives about twenty minutes from here. Was that the potentially cheating fiancé one?"

"I'm pretty sure it was. I'm almost positive the other two letters were from men."

"Good. Underneath, you can see the next name. Rafferty Jarsdel. Can't see the address, though. It's a good thing you didn't stack all three envelopes directly on top of each other."

"Well, they were opened, so they stick upwards a bit."

"Lucky us. Unfortunately, the last name's half obscured by the second envelope. Alastair N–something. Not much to go on there."

"I remember it was an unusual name. It reminded me of Agatha Christie's *And Then There Were None*."

Zabel ran a hand over her forehead. "Claythorne? Lombard? Wargrave? Armstrong? Blore? Marston? Rogers? Brent? MacArthur? None of those names begin with N!"

Just when I thought that I couldn't find her any more attractive if I tried, she knocked me for a loop by demonstrating how well she knew Agatha Christie's novel. "The ferryman! Narracott!"

"Yes! Only it wasn't Narracott. It was something like it."

"Let me work my search engine magic." Zabel mumbled as she typed. "Alastair Narracott Sherlock Holmes. And… it says… 'Do you mean "Alastair *Nithercott* Sherlock Holmes?' Turns out, he's written a couple of articles for the Alfriston Sherlock Holmes Society."

"Funny. I haven't heard of him. I know most people in the local fandoms."

"Hmm. Well, a search for "Alastair Nithercott Alfriston" gives me what I hope is his address… No phone number, though… Now for the other… I can't believe it…"

"What?"

"There are three Rafferty Jarsdels in London. I'm surprised there's even one." She kept tapping her tablet and scribbling in her notebook. "I've got their phone numbers. Only one thing to do now." Pulling out her phone, she dialed and waited. "Hello? I'm calling for Mr. Rafferty Jarsdel… Why can't I speak to him?... Oh, I'm so sorry, I had no idea… So he didn't send me a letter… Actually, do you know if he has relatives by that name? I might be mixing this Mr. Jarsdel up with one of them... He does? That explains it, thank you. Goodbye!" Ending the call, Zabel explained, "I just called an eighty-one-year-old Rafferty Jarsdel. He has a son and a grandson with that name. This man had a stroke a month ago and couldn't write a letter. I just spoke to his carer. Time for the second number.... Hello? Mr. Jarsdel? Mr. Jarsdel, Jr., father of Rafferty Jarsdel III? Yes, first of all, I want to say that I hope that your father gets well soon. I know this sounds like a silly question, but did you send a letter to a bank recently, asking Sherlock Holmes to investigate a case for you? Huh... Hello? Hello?" She looked up with an annoyed expression. "He hung up on me."

"How rude."

"Before he did, he said that he didn't send any fool letters to Sherlock bleeding Holmes, but that sounded like the kind of idiotic thing his moron son would do."

"Sounds like a warm and loving father."

"Indeed." Zabel sniffed. "I'm pretty sure I could smell the whiskey fumes on his breath through the mobile phone."

"Breakfast of champions?"

"I went out with a guy with that attitude my first week at university. We went out twice. Before I could break up with him he was sent down for lewd inebriated behavior and I never saw or heard from him again." A thoughtful yet worried expression took form across her face. "If you never properly end a relationship, is it technically still continuing?"

"I think that once a certain amount of time elapses without him sending you flowers, the relationship is automatically ended."

"Just as well, I suppose. Shall I give Rafferty Jarsdel III a call?"

"By all means."

She dialed, waited, and one ring before she gave up, a groggy "Hello?" warbled out of the speaker. After a few brief words of introduction, Zabel apologized for waking him and explained the situation. By this point, I had moved over to her side of the table and she was holding the mobile so we could both hear.

"Wait? You got my letter to Sherlock Holmes?"

"Yes."

"Damn. I never thought anybody would actually answer it. Someone really has a job answering those letters?"

"Yes, I do," I replied before I could stop myself.

Evidently Rafferty Jarsdel III didn't realize that the voice on the other end of the line had changed. "Wait? Aren't you that lady who does the true crime videos?"

"Yes, I am."

"Where are you now? Can you meet me somewhere soon?"

After a quick word of agreement, we made an appointment to meet at a coffee shop in forty-five minutes. He'd wanted us to meet him at his flat, but as Zabel told me after the call had ended that it was always a good idea to meet potential suspects in a public place.

"But you came to my flat. You waited inside while I got dressed."

"Yes, well, normally I would have waited out in the hall, but... for reasons I can't explain, I had— have a very good feeling about you." Her smile was so warm and bright that I felt like I'd accidentally gotten on a rocket ship headed straight for the sun.

"The coffee shop's half an hour away. Shall we start heading over?"

I beamed back at her. "Definitely!"

CHAPTER THREE
Rafferty Jarsdel III

When we arrived at the coffee shop, Zabel excused herself on the pretext of touching up her makeup, and asked me to order two cups of their cheapest coffee and save us some seats. This was one of those establishments that seemed to be unable to find a uniform collection of chairs, so they rushed around from one used furniture store to another, buying whatever inexpensive items they could find that fit their budget, and scattered them randomly about the room. There were a couple of wicker chairs that appeared to be capable of supporting only people who weigh sixty pounds or less, a trio of wooden benches that looked like someone sitting on them could last at most two minutes before springing to one's feet in agony, a pile of filthy bean bags in one corner, and a smattering of tables with ordinary wooden chairs around them. Fortunately, there was a cluster of four armchairs around a low circular table that looked reasonably comfortable, so as soon as I placed the order for two cups of coffee, I rushed over to those chairs and draped my coat over one and sat in another to claim them. There weren't many other people in the coffee shop, and the few patrons that were there were all staring at various electronic devices with ear buds securely in place.

Not wanting to be left out, I checked my mobile, and discovered a message from Sanna. I called her back, and a third of the way through the first ring, she answered with an excited "How'd it go?"

"It's still going, actually," I replied, quickly bringing her up to speed.

"What did she eat at breakfast?" Sanna asked. After I provided a quick description of her meal, Sanna followed up with the question, "Did she eat all of it, or did she just nibble at it?"

"She ate it all."

"Hmm."

"What's that supposed to mean?"

"That's not a good sign, Addy."

"What do you mean?"

"Look, I think it's pretty safe to say that your preferred relationship status with this woman is not going to be platonic buddy."

"I'm aware that my feelings are obvious and I'm hoping that she finds my transparency charming."

"Your optimism is inspiring, Addy. But if you'll forgive me for saying so, you're not the best at reading cues. When certain types of women are attracted to a man and want to impress him– and I have strong reason to suspect that Zabel is that type of woman– they make a big show of not eating very much in front of that man. If she eats normally, even heavily, that means that she's comfortable around the guy, sees no reason to impress him, and that mentally she has relegated him to the friend zone."

A memory popped into my brain. "The first time you and I started hanging out, you insisted we have dinner at a new all you can eat buffet."

"That's right, and I got my money's worth. But now that you and I know each other pretty thoroughly, you'll realize that you have no reason to take it personally."

This was true, and I didn't take any offense at all. After a moment's reflection, I added, "Well, it wasn't a very big plate of poached eggs. Just two smallish ones, along with little heaps of avocado and tomato."

"Did the meal come with toast and potatoes?"
"No, it didn't."

The brief intake of breath from Sanna buoyed my optimism. "Oh. That's actually very promising."

"And the owners of the restaurant are friends of hers, and they might have been upset if she didn't eat her food."

"Well if that's the case, you're not down and out just yet. Wait a minute. How did she explain her absence just now? Did she use the words "bathroom," "loo," or "toilet?""

"No, she just said she needed to touch up her mascara."

There was another oddly encouraging intake of breath from Sanna. "A flimsy euphemism. That's excellent. A woman like Zabel, when she might be attracted to a man, doesn't like to admit that she has actual bodily functions. She's made no mention whatsoever of her menses?"

"None whatsoever. Do I need to ask for clarification on that last question?"

"Nah, you can figure out the significance yourself. Addy, you mustn't get overconfident–"

"Never do."

"–But you could actually have a chance with her. Don't overthink it, and don't wimp out."

"I won't." As I said this, Zabel emerged from the restroom. "She's coming back."

"Best of luck to you. Remember, before you say or do anything in front of her, always ask yourself, 'What would someone much cooler and confident than me do?'"

"That's sound advice."

"I'll be cheering you on from work. Call me again if there are any more developments."

As I slid my mobile back into my coat pocket, I belatedly remembered that I should rise as Zabel approached, and I did just as she reached the cluster of chairs. A flicker of a smile raised my spirits. While I'd been on the phone with Sanna, the waitress had deposited two cups of their plain coffee in front of us. Zabel glanced at her beverage but made no attempt to touch it. When I inquired into her disinterest, she explained, "It's awful. I could tell right away when we walked inside. Based on the smell, it's terrible coffee."

"So why did you ask me to order two cups?"

"Because I've learned from experience that when I interview somebody I've never met before who might or might not be involved in a crime, or is male, it helps to have something handy for self-defense purposes. And given all the rules and regulations these days that can get you arrested if you carry anything that could be even remotely be considered as a weapon, the perfect object to keep handy is a cup of hot liquid. Over the years, I've learned how to spill it strategically and make it look accidental."

"Ah." With that, I made a mental note to stay on my best behavior, but I couldn't help myself from taking a sip. I couldn't tell whether my cup contained coffee or the dishwater used to clean the mug.

"Told you," Zabel said with no hint of triumph.

"How does this place stay in business?"

"There are some unsolved mysteries that even I'm not interested in investigating. If you want to have one of those sugar lumps, go right ahead."

I declined and then immediately thought better of it and helped myself. Just as my mouth felt pleasant again, Zabel looked over at the door and said, "That's him" and waved Rafferty over to us.

I felt rather sorry for Rafferty Jarsdel III the moment I laid eyes on him, as it appeared that he had no one in his life who cared about him enough to tell him that his attempts at facial hair were not his finest idea. His jeans looked as if they were about a year overdue for an appointment with some hot water and detergent, and altogether he seemed to be trying to cultivate an aesthetic that just wasn't the least bit flattering to him.

After a few minutes of fawning over Zabel and telling her how much he liked her work, Rafferty looked down at our cups and grimaced. "You didn't order the coffee, did you?"

"We all make mistakes," I replied.

"I know it's a coffee shop, but you should stick to the tea here. The pastry isn't half bad either."

A little nudge from Zabel gave me the hint that I should offer to pay for his tea and scone, and as I was about to rise and follow Rafferty to the glass case where he was selecting from today's assortment of baked goods, Zabel whispered in my ear, "I'll reimburse you, don't worry."

I wasn't sure if Zabel thought my financial situation was so precarious that I couldn't afford to buy somebody a cup of tea and a scone, but this wasn't the time to ask her further questions. When we returned, Rafferty sank his teeth into an apricot-thyme scone and sighed. "So, why are you so interested in that little letter I sent to Sherlock Holmes?"

I told him the story of the robbery. At times, he almost looked interested.

"That's weird. I don't know why anybody would've been interested in my letter. It was of no interest to anybody but me."

"Why did you write to the bank?" Zabel asked.

"Ah." Rafferty chewed more scone. "Well, you see, a couple of days ago, I was faced with a problem and I was rather frazzled, so I took something to take the edge off. You're recording this, aren't you?"

"Yes. Just for notetaking purposes. Do you mind?"

"No, but in case that recording ever falls into the hands of the police, I shall say that in order to help myself relax, I drank a few perfectly legal beers. So, after those... *beers*... I wasn't thinking as clearly as I often do, and somewhere along the way I got the idea that it would be a good idea to ask Sherlock Holmes for help. I think there was an old Basil Rathbone movie on the telly at that moment, so that's probably what gave my addled mind the idea. So I sat down, dashed off an appeal for help to the great detective, and posted it on my way to the corner shop to buy a bag each of prawn, beef and mustard, ham

56

and pickle, onion and balsamic, red pepper, and horseradish cheddar crisps." He smiled. "My cravings were a bit severe that night."

I cast my mind back to the contents of the letter. I couldn't remember his correspondence word for word, but I did recall that his writing had taken the lines on his stationary as a suggestion and not a rule. I also recalled a higher than usual proportion of spelling and punctuation errors, but I'm hired to respond to the letters, not to mark them up with a red pen until all of their effronteries to accepted standards of grammar have been identified and shamed.

"I'm surprised that you can remember your crisp shopping list," Zabel noted. She was making the same look that Sanna makes whenever she's developed a strong dislike and distrust for somebody else, but for various reasons can't come right out and call out that person for not meeting her high standards.

"Actually, I buy the same order a couple of times a week, so I'm very familiar with it." Rafferty took another bite of scone and tried to wipe away the crumbs from his beard with the back of his hand. He was only one-third successful.

"Rafferty, I don't think you mentioned what exactly you wanted Sherlock Holmes to find in your letter," I noted. "I know that you said that you'd lost an item that meant a lot to you, but did you say specifically what it was?"

"No, I didn't." Rafferty sipped his tea.

Seven silent seconds passed. Zabel ran out of patience before I did. "Would you care to let us know what that item is?"

"Ah, yes..." Rafferty lifted his cup to his hairy, crumb-covered lips again. "It's a bit embarrassing, really."

"Even more embarrassing than admitting that you got yourself into a... *beer*-fueled haze and decided that it would be a nifty idea to write to Sherlock Holmes and hope he was clever enough to locate an item without your even having the courtesy to say what it was?"

If Rafferty was offended, he didn't show it. "I think I established that I wasn't at my sharpest when I wrote that letter. Indeed, part of the reason why I fell into the condition that I did is because I was is such a dither due to the traumatic events that happened to me earlier that evening."

Twin waves of curiosity and trepidation washed over me. "Could you please tell us what happened?"

"Well..." It was hard to tell if the emotions that flashed on his face were shame or smugness. Possibly a combination of the two. "Can I trust you to be discreet in your reportage, darling?"

Zabel smiled with her mouth but not with her eyes. I'd only known her for a couple of hours, but already I knew that a near-stranger referring to her as "darling" was not a shrewd move to win her good graces. "I never try to embarrass anybody who doesn't deserve it."

"Fair enough." The last remnants of the scone were shoved behind the abomination that was Rafferty's facial hair. "A couple of days ago, my wallet was stolen."

"I'm sorry to hear that." I meant that. "But why would that be embarrassing to you?"

He shrugged. "Well, you see, my wallet was in the pocket of my best pair of trousers at the time."

"Are you pulling our legs?" was my reflexive response.

"If only I were. You see, I was going for a twilight stroll through a local park. I was basking in the beauty of nature when an opportunity presented itself, and I found myself unable to resist taking advantage of it. So I did, and at a certain point in the proceedings the aforementioned garment was placed upon a nearby bush for reasons of hygiene, and a few minutes later when it came time to retrieve them, my trousers– and my wallet– were missing." He gazed at me with a slight trace of pleading in his eyes and then pivoted to Zabel. "Are you judging me?"

"Of course not. Who among us hasn't been in exactly that position?" The sarcasm that Zabel utilized at that moment was professional level. Amateurs should never try to replicate it.

"Well, as you can imagine, I was in a bit of a bind, and when an individual who I hoped would be kind enough to take on the role of good Samaritan chose to sprint away, I decided my wisest choice of action was to stay concealed amongst the shrubbery for as long as possible. I thought perhaps it might be safest to wait until the middle of the night, but when a horde of drunken men mistook my place of hiding for a public convenience, I was forced to flee. Luckily by that point, it was quite dark, and I was thanking my lucky stars that I'd happened to wear a coat that came to just above my knees. Still, I was several blocks from my flat, and I found myself advancing several yards at a time, only to duck into a dark and convenient alley when someone approached. In one of those alleys, I discovered a discarded, half-empty container of fish vindaloo at the top of a rubbish bin, and my admittedly not dazzlingly bright idea was to smear the curry upon my pale and bony legs as a means of disguising my condition."

"And did it work?"

He sighed. "It was the fish scent, I suppose, that caught the attention of approximately seven hundred cats, some more feral than others. I was never much of a sprinter, but I made it back to my flat in record time, cleaned myself up, and took the necessary measures to calm myself down. Having done that, I told you the state of mind I was in when I wrote the letter to Sherlock Holmes and purchased my crisps."

After all of that, I was disposed to be sympathetic. "You certainly had a difficult evening."

"Indeed, I did. Though truth to tell, it was far from my most embarrassing moment of the week." He spread out his hands. "And that's it. I doubt you'll be able to find my trousers and wallet, but it was worth a shot."

"You wouldn't happen to have a picture of the trousers in question to assist in tracking them down, would you?" I asked.

"Actually, yes." Rafferty fiddled with his mobile, asked for my contact information, and sent me a posed picture of himself sitting on a park bench with one hand on his chin and the other on his knee. He was wearing a pair of dark green trousers with a thin red plaid pattern woven into the fabric. They were distinctive, but I hadn't seen anybody wearing them lately.

"Do you have any more questions? I just remember that I have an audition across town in just under an hour, so I need to prepare." Zabel and I looked at each other, and when neither of us could come up with anything to say, Rafferty leapt to his feet, gave us an exaggerated bow, shook both our hands, and made his departure.

"He seems to be a bit of a character," Zabel said as soon as the coffee shop door slammed shut.

"You clearly didn't like him."

"He reminds me of my youngest sister's ex-boyfriend. She's not the hairdresser, this is a different sibling. He thinks he's charming, but he keeps finding himself in one hot mess of a situation after another, leaving the person closest to him to clean up everything for him." She shuddered. "No job, poor hygiene, and very proud of the fact that none of his six arrests led to convictions."

"At least your sister broke up with him."

"Actually, he dumped her for someone even younger– he's fifteen years older than my sister, by the way. And her new boyfriend is a good deal handsomer but no better on the inside." Zabel's entire body quivered. "My aunt tells me to focus on my own personal life. Worry about finding a boyfriend for myself rather than fretting over my sister's."

Zabel talked for a bit after that, but all I could hear were the words *She's single!* rattling around my brain. My mind finally quieted down in time to hear her say, "I don't see why anybody would've wanted to steal that letter, do you?"

"No, I don't. Of course, there could be something we missed, but I can't think of anything."

"Then perhaps–" Zabel's phone chimed. "Hang on, I've got a text… It's Lacina Berrycloth. I looked up her phone number a little while ago when

63

I left you alone, and I texted her about her letter. She just texted me back and said she'd be happy to meet with us. She asked us if we could meet her at the bookstore across the street from her workplace. Sounds all right to me. Are you still willing to come along?"

"Absolutely!" I probably put ten times more enthusiasm than I should've into that response, so I toned it down when I added, "I mean, I certainly don't have anything more interesting to do."

"Excellent." And with that, we left the coffee shop to meet Lacina Berrycloth.

CHAPTER FOUR
Lacina Berrycloth

When we reached the bookstore, Zabel texted Lacina to let her know we'd arrived. Moments later, a woman with a shaggy blonde pixie cut and a dandelion-yellow pantsuit dashed out of the office building across the street and into the bookstore. But it wasn't her hair and clothes that were the first thing I noticed about her: It was her eyes. A few weeks earlier, I'd run into a homeless woman whose face was so filthy it was impossible to tell her age. She looked enormous, but that was mostly because she was wearing an entire department store's worth of clothing, and she had grey hair that hadn't been cut or washed since at least two prime ministers ago. I'd tried to avoid her, but she latched onto me and sprinted over and asked me for money, but she inquired if I had any American dollars prior to 1996, because all other paper currency worldwide produced after that date contained tracking devices that the secret world government used to monitor our every action. When I was unable to provide her with the type of cash she desired, she thanked me anyway, dropped to the ground, kissed the tops of both my shoes, and excused herself, telling me that the squirrels were spying on her and that I should watch out for them too, because they were treacherous liars.

Lacina Berrycloth had exactly the same eyes as that homeless woman.

I didn't have time to weigh my options. Before I could say a word to Zabel, Lacina rushed up to us with surprising speed. After greeting us by name and shaking our hands with sufficient vigor to fracture our wrists, she fixed a gaze upon us that I tried to break away from but failed. "So Sherlock Holmes couldn't come himself?"

Zabel and I exchanged a glance that wordlessly told me that our thoughts about Lacina were on the same page. "No, he can't," I finally said, "because—"

Before I could complete my sentence with the words "he's a fictional character and I just answer mail addressed to him," Lacina cut in with "I know. He's probably very busy and he's dealing with other cases. I'll bet the government overwhelms him with one problem after another."

"How old do you think he is?" were the words that slipped out of my mouth before I could consider her potential reactions.

In any event, she didn't seem to hear me. "I know the romantic life of an ordinary woman doesn't matter much to a great man like Mr. Holmes, but I am desperate. You received my letter, right?"

"Yes, but it was stolen."

"Stolen! Are you saying that some criminal knows about my suspicions about my boyfriend?"

My tongue suddenly lost its flexibility, and when it became clear that I wouldn't be able to contribute a coherent response, Zabel stepped in, saying, "I'm afraid so. Can you please give us some more details? It might help us figure out who took it and get the letter back."

Lacina's breath quickened, and after running her hands through her hair, she nodded. "All right. I don't remember the exact words of my letter. I only know that I was worried my fiancé was seeing someone else."

I hadn't done such fast mental calculations since that time when I was seventeen and I was desperately trying to wrap up the last question on the calculus exam before my teacher called time. All of my instincts told me that Ms. Berrycloth would not take kindly to any attempts to inform her that I didn't actually work for Sherlock Holmes and that there was absolutely no chance that Holmes could possibly help her. "Mr. Holmes only investigates actual crimes–"

"This is a crime!" I could see the fury burning in her eyes. "Playing with my heart is a crime!"

At this point, I could feel the eyes of every person in the bookstore upon us. I could be wrong, but I'm pretty sure I saw a lot of sympathy, but also a great deal of fear– fear that they might be drawn into this conversation. A queue hurriedly started forming by the cashier.

"Maybe it would be better if I went back to Baker Street with you," Lacina added. "I'd love to get a look inside 221B."

From the expression on Zabel's face, she agreed with me in my assessment that it was not the wisest course of action to inform her that it was physically impossible to visit Sherlock Holmes' home.

"Mr. Holmes retired and moved away from 221B long ago, didn't you know?" Zabel informed her. "He left London and his consulting detective practice in order to focus on bee farming in the Sussex Downs."

There are no words to explain the rush of endorphins that coursed through my brain as Zabel demonstrated her knowledge of Sherlock Holmes' later years. I didn't have time to bask in the wondrousness that was her very long before Lacina cut in with evident irritation. "Don't give me that! You know damn well he's much too young to retire!"

The synapses of my brain went into overdrive, and I realized with unnerving swiftness that Ms. Berrycloth was thinking of a contemporary television adaptation of Holmes. From the confused and concerned looks of the various bookstore employees, they didn't recognize her, which meant that she wasn't a regular patron of the store even though it was right across the street from her workplace. This led to the fairly solid conclusion that she was not a dedicated reader.

Zabel and I were standing against a bookcase, so we were incapable of taking a step back as Lacina moved towards us, despite our desire to keep a reasonable distance between us. Her voice rang out high and shrill. "I need Sherlock Holmes to find out what's going on with my fiancé! He's the only person who can help me!"

One of the cashiers, who had been casting a wary eye in our direction since Lacina entered, finally plucked up enough courage to break his stony silence. "Is everything all right over there?" he called out without actually taking a step in our direction.

"Everything's fine! Shut up and go back to your books!" Lacina's response was so sharp and fierce that the poor cashier never considered that he should intervene further. After hastily wrapping up the purchase of the last customer in line, he dabbed his forehead with a handkerchief and beat a hasty retreat to a back room.

By this point, Lacina was right in our faces, and I could see the little red marks caused by burst capillaries in her eyes. I couldn't be certain, but it was quite possible that the damage had been done by excessive shouting and unrestrained tantrums. That happened with a family member of mine whom I won't identify here.

"My fiancé is a great guy," Lacina hissed. "A very handsome guy. An incredibly successful guy. A very charming guy. Everything's been going great. But now something's wrong. He's lying to me. He's been cancelling dates at a moment's notice. He's been making ridiculous excuses not to swing by my flat several nights a week. He's not as… attentive to my needs as he used to be. And now, last week, I found this on his suit!" She pulled an envelope out of her inner jacket pocket.

"Is there a hair inside that envelope?" I asked.

"Yes! How did you know?"

"Well it seemed reasonable. You said you found something on his suit, and you're holding up that envelope, which looks pretty flat to me, which indicates that whatever's in there is small and thin. And anyway, what might you find on a suit that indicates cheating? A hair seems like the most likely item. Probably much longer than yours or a different color. Maybe both."

"Yes!" The anger faded from her face. "Oh, I can tell you've been working with Sherlock Holmes. You've picked up some wonderful observational skills from him!" Technically, that was true, just not in the way she was thinking. It's amazing how you can improve your observational powers just by reading Sherlock Holmes stories. She pulled a very long black hair from the envelope. "See! See!"

"But that doesn't mean anything," Zabel noted. "It's so easy for someone to pick up a hair from someone else. Maybe he just bumped into somebody on the street and the hair transferred. It could happen."

Lacina's eyes narrowed into suspicious slits, and she held the hair up to Zabel's head. "You know... this hair looks like it could be one of yours... Have you met my fiancé?"

"I don't even know who he is!" Zabel gasped.

I decided to play fast and loose with the truth in order to defuse the situation. "Ms. Berrycloth, Zabel and I work very closely together, and I can assure you she hasn't had any time to date lately, so she couldn't possibly be seeing your fiancé."

The agitation in Lacina's face started fading again. "Oh. Right, right. Thousands of women have hair like this. No reason why it might be you." The iron re-entered her voice, and the volume of her tone started rising. "But when I find that little trollop, I swear I'm going to–"

"Darling? Is everything all right?"

A tall man with blond hair and a shiny suit walked up to us. I distrusted him immediately. A man who wears clothes that cost more than I make in two years must have something shady about him.

Instantaneously, Lacina's voice grew softer and her manner became kittenish. "Sweetie-pie!"

Waving her hand from the new arrival to us, she introduced us, "This is my fiancé, Prescott. Prescott, this is Zabel and Andy."

"Addy," I corrected.

"Pleased to meet you." After the standard shaking of hands, Prescott said, "Darling, people are looking for you. It's time for your presentation."

"What? Oh, yes. Sorry, I just had to talk to these two. They're very interesting. They work with Sherlock Holmes, you know." Prescott looked confused, but before he said anything, Lacina threw her arms around him, planted a kiss on his lips, and scurried out of the bookstore. The cashiers relaxed visibly as she crossed the street to her workplace.

Prescott shot us a suspicious look. "What did she mean about your working for Sherlock Holmes?"

After a hurried explanation from me, Prescott broke out into peals of laughter. "That's Lacina. She has... trouble determining the line between fact and fiction sometimes." He gestured towards some chairs in the corner, and we all sat down.

Smoothing out his ridiculously expensive suit, Prescott asked, "So why did she call you here? Did she want to hire you? But why would she want to hire you? Unless... did she ask you to investigate me? Does she think that I'm cheating on her or something?"

Neither of us answered, but apparently we didn't need to, because our faces provided the response. "I see." Prescott leaned back in his chair. "It's all a misunderstanding. I know I haven't been there for her as much as I should be lately, but there's a reason for that. I'm making plans for an around-the-world trip for our honeymoon, and I have to duck out and meet with my travel agents in order to set up the details."

It sounded reasonable enough at first, but after thinking about it for half a second I became suspicious. Most people set up their travel plans through the Internet these days, and if Prescott was such a big business big shot, wouldn't he have an assistant who could handle the travel plans?

Prescott fumbled around his pocket and produced a glossy leather wallet. "Let me reimburse you for your time," he said, extracting a handful of bills.

"Oh no, we couldn't..." Zabel said. "Isn't that right, Addy?"

I didn't say anything. My attention was fixed on a mark on the leather of Prescott's wallet. "What's the matter, Addy?" Zabel asked.

"Look at his wallet, Zabel. He's got the adulterer's circle."

"The adulterer's circle?" Prescott repeated with a chuckle. "What's that?"

"When married men want to appear to be single, a lot of them stick their wedding rings into a slit in their wallets. If they do it regularly, the ring puts pressure on the delicate leather, leaving an indentation. The adulterer's circle. In fact..." I reached into his wallet and pulled out a little piece of gold jewelry. Reading the inscription aloud, I said, "E to P. All my love." Is E. your wife? Elizabeth? Emily? Evelyn?"

Prescott sagged. "Edith," he replied.

"Huh. So Lacina was right. You are seeing another woman, but she's your wife. Lacina's the mistress, only she doesn't know it. Are you planning to become a bigamist?"

I was expecting more equivocation, but Prescott had fallen into confession mode. "Not legally. I've been mulling my options, and I've been considering having a friend claim to have been ordained on the Internet perform the ceremony, only he hasn't, so it wouldn't be legal."

"So you want to fake-marry Lacina?" Zabel, who moments earlier had been unnerved by Lacina, was now firmly on her side.

"You don't understand! I love her! But I also love Edith. And our children."

"Does Edith have long black hair?" I asked.

"What? No. It's long, but it's auburn."

"Lacina's suspicions went into overdrive when she saw a long black hair on your suit."

"Oh." It was lucky that Prescott wasn't a spy, because if he ever got captured by the enemy, he'd be spilling our nation's secrets in thirty seconds flat. "That's Okita's."

"Is she your other girlfriend?" Zabel asked, doing her best impression of a polar vortex.

"No, not exactly. She's my other wife. They don't know about each other."

I heard a faint but high-pitched wail emanating from Prescott's trousers. For a moment I thought that the suit was so expensive that it could feel actual pain if its wearer was sitting in such a manner that it caused the cloth to wrinkle, but then I deduced the true cause. "Is that your mobile?"

Prescott reached into his suit and withdrew his mobile. As he stared at the screen, the blood drained from his face. "I think you accidentally pocket dialed someone when you reached for your wallet," I explained a tad redundantly. "Who did you call?"

A bright yellow blur tearing across the street and into the bookstore informed me that he had inadvertently told Lacina about her competition for his attentions. "You're married? *TWICE?*"

Hell, it is well known, hath no fury like a woman who has just discovered that her fiancé has two other wives. I cannot explain what Prescott said next, as his sudden stammer rendered his words unintelligible. Lacina's replies were loud, high, and profane. Zabel and I were just in the process of slipping out when Lacina suddenly grabbed an armful of thick hardcover books from the shelf beside her, and started throwing them at the cringing bigamist. Unfortunately, some of the books started bouncing off of him and deflected in my general direction.

As Zabel and I made our retreat, one of the cashiers informed us that she was calling the police. "That's an excellent idea," Zabel replied. "Please do so right away."

While we slipped out the door, Zabel told me, "We definitely don't want to be around when the police arrived. There's always a chance that we could be detained as witnesses or even arrested or cautioned ourselves, and we don't want to waste any valuable time."

"No, we do not." By this point, we were in her car. "So," I mused as we drove away, "I don't think Lacina's letter was the reason why the robbers broke into my office yesterday. Prescott didn't seem interested in it, even though he had a motive to keep her from finding out that he was not a single man."

"I agree. Maybe one of his wives would've had a motive to steal the letter, but I doubt it. Why go through all that trouble to keep your husband's latest girlfriend from finding out the truth? Heck, if I were his wife, I'd want her to know. It doesn't make sense to me."

"Right. Which means that the only letter left is Alastair Nithercott's."

"We don't have his phone number, but his home is a little over two hours' drive away. Do you want to take the chance and head over there in the hopes that he's at home?"

My response was a hearty and unconditional "yes." Over the course of the drive, we chatted and discovered we had very similar tastes in music and entertainment, and similar opinions on all sorts of make-or-break issues, and I was finding it increasingly difficult to play it cool, as my infatuation was reaching levels that I had not achieved since the more embarrassing years of puberty.

The next two hours and fifteen minutes passed swiftly, and very soon we were in Alfriston. It took a little while to find Mr. Nithercott's cottage, but after three wrong turns, we came to the correct address.

"I hope we didn't come all this way for nothing," Zabel remarked as she climbed out of the car. "For all we know, he's at work and we'll have a long wait until he gets back."

"Yes, we'll just have to see." In my heart, I was hoping that we would have to stick around Alfriston waiting for him, just so Zabel and I could be assured of more time together.

Before we could even ring the bell, a frazzled-looking woman dressed entirely in faded blue denim stepped out of the house, carrying a cardboard box filled with assorted papers. "Hello!" Zabel said brightly. "Is this the home of Alastair Nithercott?"

"It used to be," the woman with the cardboard box replied. "I'm his great-niece, Rhoda. Can I help you?"

We introduced ourselves, and asked where Mr. Nithercott was. "What do you mean, it "used to be" his house?" I asked.

"Well, I'm sorry to tell you this, but Great-Uncle Alastair is dead. He was murdered yesterday morning."

CHAPTER FIVE
Great-Uncle Alastair's Obsessions

Zabel and I both had the sensation of having a large glass of ice-cold water poured down our backs.

"He's dead?" Zabel gasped.

"And you said he was murdered?" I added, as if I weren't already one hundred percent sure of what Rhoda had said. I was just too surprised to come up with anything cleverer or more insightful at the moment.

"That's right," Rhoda nodded. She looked a bit sad, but not devastated.

"Why didn't my Internet search bring that up?" Zabel wondered, more to herself than anybody else.

"I just found out about it an hour ago," Rhoda explained. "It wasn't an obvious murder. They didn't know how he died until after the autopsy."

Managing a tiny bit of decorum, I forced myself to add the words, "I'm so sorry. This must be terrible for you," before asking, "How did he die?"

"Someone smothered him yesterday morning." After a quarter of a second's pause, Rhoda added with a considerable amount of defensiveness,

"I had nothing to do with it, by the way. I was at home in Bristol, and I was having lunch with plenty of witnesses around when Great-Uncle Alastair died."

I thought about an apologetic "We weren't accusing you…" but truth to tell, the moment I heard the word "murdered," I wondered if she'd had anything to do with it, based on no evidence whatsoever save for her connection to the victim. Instead of trying to placate her, I pressed forward. "If he was murdered, are you allowed to take anything away from the house?"

"What?" Rhoda looked down, as if she'd forgotten she was carrying the box. "Oh, yes. I'm going to set this down if we're going to talk." She placed the box on a nearby stone wall and continued. "These are Great-Uncle Alastair's papers. I need to get them to his solicitor to start the necessary formalities going. I have every right to be here, you know. My brother and sister and I are Great-Uncle Alastair's heirs."

I was a bit confused. "So he wasn't killed here in this house? This isn't a crime scene?"

"What? No. Why would you think he was murdered here?"

"You said "smothered." The first image that popped into my mind was him lying in bed, and somebody pressed a pillow over his face."

"Oh, I see. No, he was killed at the local library. They found him in an easy chair in a quiet reading nook, and everybody thought he'd just passed away suddenly. It was very inconvenient, because it was story time for the young children, and you can't very well read a group of little kids *James and the Giant Peach* when there's an elderly man lying dead just ten feet away."

I nodded. "It's the sort of thing that could scar impressionable young minds."

"Mm-hmm. They took him away as soon as they could, but once the doctors looked over him, they found bruising and other signs of a struggle. They think someone pressed something over his face– there weren't any pillows around, but maybe a thick coat or something like that– and held it over his face until he died." Rhoda shuddered. "Terrible. He was such a nice man. I don't know why anybody would do that to him." She turned to Zabel. "The police just told me about their discovery this morning. It hasn't had time to make the news yet."

"I see. Do the police have any suspects yet?" Zabel asked.

"No. Not that you said anything, but my siblings are both out of the country, so they had nothing to do with it. Like I said, he was a loveable man. No one could possibly have any reason to hurt him. The librarian and the kids who were there for story time aren't really suspects, but they were in the front hall for a while waiting for people to come, and there's a side door. It's possible that's somebody else could've just slipped in and killed poor Great-Uncle Alastair, but why?"

"Can you tell us anything about him?"

Rhoda's eyes narrowed at me. "Any dark secrets or terrible rumours about him, you mean?"

"No!" My vehemence made her jump a bit, and I think I convinced her that I had absolutely no intention of soiling her great-uncle's memory. "I just want to know more about the man who sent a letter to Sherlock Holmes earlier this week."

"Wait, what?"

At this point, I was compelled to tell her the whole story of the robbery, the stolen letters, and our investigation. Ten minutes later, Rhoda, now knowing why we were making these inquiries, was looking at us far more warmly.

"And that's why you came down here and started asking me these questions?"

"Yes." Zabel had to field that question. I was a trifle out of breath after recapping the events of the last twenty-four hours.

"You say it was about some sort of lost Sherlock Holmes movie?"

"Uh-huh. I only had the time to scan the letter, so I don't remember much of it."

"Wait a minute." Rhoda fished a car fob out of her jeans pocket and clicked it. "Put that box in the boot for me, please, and then come inside."

I complied, and when I returned, I found that Rhoda and Zabel were both inside the cottage. I followed the sound of their voices to a little table by a large window, with a computer and printer upon it.

"Luckily, Great-Uncle Alastair gave me his password, just in case anything happened to him. My brother gave me the password to his personal computer as well, with the strict instructions to delete his browser history without looking at it, and whatever I do, don't let his wife see the websites he's been viewing."

I know it's bad etiquette, but I watched the keys Rhoda typed for the password– "D0cWats0n." Not the most secure password, but as Rhoda informed us, Great-Uncle Alastair was pushing ninety and it just didn't make sense to use anything too challenging to remember.

Rhoda clicked on a folder labelled RECENT CORRESPONDENCE. "Here we are. You say that you received the letter yesterday?"

"That's right."

"Here we go. The last letter he ever wrote, apparently. Written two days ago, and yes... it's addressed to 221B Baker Street."

She printed out the letter, and as soon as she handed it to me, I started reading it aloud. To reiterate, I hadn't read it thoroughly when I'd opened the envelope, I'd only scanned it quickly in order to determine which pile to sort it into, so I'd missed the lion's share of the message.

Dear Whoever Is Answering This in Sherlock Holmes' Name:

Greetings! My name is Alastair Nithercott, and I am quite aware that I am not actually writing to Mr. Sherlock Holmes. I am fully aware that whoever is reading this is a bank employee tasked with answering a wide variety of questions about Sherlock Holmes and his cases, and I wouldn't be surprised if people wrote to you with actual cases to solve.

"Right on the money, Mr. Nithercott," I murmured before continuing onwards.

I am writing because I am hoping that you are an expert in Sherlock Holmes, and despite all of my research, I have not come across any information that can answer my questions. Therefore, it is my fervent desire that you can provide me with much-needed answers.

As a die-hard fan of Sherlock Holmes, I have tried to watch every film production featuring the great detective. One has unfortunately eluded me. It's a one-hour television movie from November 22, 1963, titled "The Deadly Deerstalker." Though details on the movie are scarce, I found one newspaper article from that time period with the following description. "When the world's greatest detective falls ill, he quickly deduces that he's been poisoned. Someone has sprinkled a toxic substance into his favorite hat, and when Sherlock Holmes put it on, a massive dose of poison was absorbed through his scalp. Dr. Watson informs him that if he doesn't find an antidote within twenty-four hours, he's doomed. Holmes must solve the double mystery of who's trying to kill him and how to reverse the poison's effects before it's too late!"

This is clearly not based on any canonical Sherlock Holmes story, though it may have been inspired by the 1949 film noir "D.O.A." which tells the story of a poisoned man trying to solve his own murder before he succumbs. I can find very little information about it on the Internet. I've managed to find out that Declan LeCeil played Holmes and Silas Crumpet was Watson, but aside from the director being named Judson Gaspard, I have no more information. I cannot track down any recordings of the movie or any stills of it. Indeed, I'm not entirely sure that the movie was broadcast at all, due to its date of release. If you know your American history, you'll realize that the production was scheduled to be released on the day of President John F. Kennedy's assassination, and it's possible that the movie was preempted. If so, I can find no evidence of a rescheduling.

And so, I'm writing to you to ask if you know anything at all about this movie. The slightest bit of information would be deeply appreciated. Thank you very much!

Sincerely,
Alastair Nithercott

There was a short pause before Rhoda said, "That was probably the last letter that my uncle ever wrote." She snatched a tissue from a little box on the corner of the table and dabbed her eyes.

After a respectful silence, Zabel turned to me. "Are your sure that's the letter you received yesterday?"

"I think so. I told you, I only scan the letters when I open them so I can sort them into piles, and then I read them more thoroughly. Of course, sometimes I misread or miss something, and organize it wrong, but it doesn't really matter. I just arrange them as I do because the bank likes me to keep statistics on what sort of letters we receive. I'm not sure why– I don't know if they've ever used them or anything like that."

"Huh. But this is probably the letter?"

"Yes. I remember the phrases "film production" and "one-hour television movie." I didn't read too much further than that." A thought popped into my head. "Of course, if someone hacked into his computer and changed the letter in some way, there's no way I'd know."

Zabel leaned over the keyboard and clicked a bit. "The last time the letter's file was modified was in the early afternoon two days ago. Just enough time to mail it and get it to you. No one came in here after the murder to change the letter. Maybe they never thought to check it… or maybe they couldn't get it inside here. Were there any signs of a break-in? Any splintering around the door?"

Rhoda shook her head. "Nothing like that. You can check."

I did. "I don't see anything. But there are so many windows in this place, anybody could get in by smashing the glass. No reason why someone couldn't get in if they didn't want to do so."

"And if someone was really desperate to destroy the computer file, and they weren't afraid of breaking the law, why not indulge in a little bit of arson, if you didn't mind getting rid of the house as well as the computer?"

The indignant expression returned to Rhoda's face. "Are you suspecting me again? Because I wouldn't destroy my own inheritance?"

"We never suspected you in the first place," I said, not entirely truthfully. I hadn't seriously thought she'd done anything criminal, but a lifetime of reading mysteries has taught me to cast a wary eye on everybody. "Besides, if you'd been behind the letter theft, you'd never have shown us this." *Unless you changed the letter and gave us the altered version to lead us down the wrong track*, I thought to myself but didn't say. Then I remembered the time stamp on the last update to the file. A moment later, I realized that a simple alteration to the computer's clock could have reset the time stamp. "Anyway, you had a key and could have let yourself in to check the computer. No need to burn the place down." I smiled at her in a manner that I hoped didn't reveal that though I was ninety-nine percent sure that she'd had nothing to do with the letter theft, but there was still that nagging one percent that I couldn't dismiss just yet.

Rhoda started to give me a searching look, as if she were trying to detect any trace of suspicion in my mind, but Zabel interrupted her attempt to read my mind. "We can't rule out the possibility that whoever killed your great-uncle might come back for the computer. You should call the police and tell them to pick it up and put it in evidence for safekeeping. Come to think of it, why haven't they been to the house yet to search it?"

After a shrug, Rhoda replied, "The police's theory of the crime as far as I know is that someone wandered in to the library, noticed Great-Uncle Alastair sleeping, and thought that a dozing elderly man would be easy prey for a pickpocket. Then when he woke up when the thief was trying to extract his wallet, he started to scream. The thief panicked and put a hand and a handkerchief over Great-Uncle Alastair's face to quiet him, and there was a struggle and the thief accidentally held on too long and smothered him."

"Was his wallet missing?" Zabel asked.

"Yes. So was his watch."

"A gold wristwatch with a round dial?" I asked.

Rhoda nodded, and looked a little stunned, as if I'd just pulled off a stunning bit of Holmes-like deduction. "That's right. How did you know?"

I picked up an ebony bowl on a bookshelf. "Because it's in here. Along with a wallet." I handed the bowl to a considerably less-impressed Rhoda, who rifled through the contents of the bowl, which also contained a few handfuls of coins, a handkerchief, a mobile, and a Swiss Army Knife. "I guess he just left his watch and wallet at home."

Setting the bowl down on the table, Rhoda nodded. "He was always forgetting things. He was always leaving his keys behind and coming home to realize that he'd left his door unlocked. Or a restaurant would call him back to let him know he'd left his credit card there."

"Hmm. Did he have his keys with him when he died?"

"Yes. Along with a pen and a little pad of paper. Nothing else. That's all they showed me at the morgue."

"So that calls the 'pickpocket getting violent' theory into question," I mused.

"Not necessarily," Zabel re-entered the conversation. "What if someone rifled through his pockets, not knowing that he'd left his valuables at home?" I saw the justice in her observation as she added. "You should probably let the police know that they can stop looking for the watch at pawn shops and cancel anything they're doing to track the credit cards, too."

Rhoda agreed. "I'll call them as soon as I'm finished helping you. Do you have any more questions?"

"Is there anybody who might have had a reason to wish your great-uncle ill?" Zabel asked.

"Not as far as I know. I think I said before that he was a loveable man. He could annoy some people going on and on about his obsessions, but no one would kill him for boring them with his ramblings. They'd just make some excuse and walk away."

"What obsessions are you talking about?" I wondered.

"Well, Sherlock Holmes, or course. Unsolved historical crimes like Jack the Ripper and the Charles Bravo poisoning case. Victorian-era forensic science. Interesting enough if you're into that sort of thing, but a lot of people couldn't care less."

"He must have really known a lot about Sherlock Holmes," I noted. "Not to brag, but I'm pretty much an expert on everything connected to Sir Arthur Conan Doyle, and I've never heard of *The Deadly Deerstalker*."

"Oh, he's loved Sherlock Holmes ever since he was a child, and things connected to Holmes have been his passion for nearly all his life. In fact... follow me please."

We tagged along behind her, and as soon as we stepped into a little room in the back of the house I was immediately overwhelmed with jealousy. I thought I'd built up a nice little collection of Sherlock Holmes memorabilia. Great-Uncle Alastair's obsessions clearly overwhelmed mine. Ten huge shelves filled with books. Costumes hanging on portable racks. All sorts of artwork, Holmes-related objects, and memorabilia. Rhoda waved her hand. "That chair's from the Jeremy Brett television series. That lamp was in a stage production starring William Gillette. That microphone was used for broadcasts of the radio series with Basil Rathbone and Nigel Bruce."

"What's going to happen to all of this?" I asked, hoping the bank would lose its business sense and agree to fund a massive purchase.

"According to Great-Uncle Alastair's will, it's all going to his friends at the Alfriston Sherlock Holmes Society. The two of them can fight over all of this themselves."

"There were only three people in the group?"

"Oh, yes. They'd meet up once or twice a week at a local pub and talk. Sometimes they'd come over to one another's houses to watch an adaptation or something like that."

"Hmm." I only half-heard what Rhoda was saying, because I was wondering if either of the two surviving members of the Alfriston Sherlock Holmes Society would be willing to sell a portion of their inheritance cheap. It was at that point that another suspicion popped into my head. *This is a nice collection... but is it nice enough for someone to kill for it?*

While I was suspecting two people I'd never met and didn't even know the names of, Zabel was circling back to the letter. "Did your great-uncle ever say anything about that television production to you?"

"It's possible he mentioned it at dinner sometime, but I have three children who require a lot of attention, so it's quite likely that something was said and just didn't register."

"And you don't know of anything else that might be connected to the contents of this letter?"

"No. But maybe one of his friends can help."

"And they are?"

"Agrona Lowell. She's a retired restaurant chef. And Wren Bevan. He's a pensioner, but I haven't a clue what he used to do for a living."

"Do you have their phone numbers or addresses?"

"Great-Uncle Alastair kept a little black book in one of his desk drawers..."

Rhoda rummaged around for a couple of minutes, but just as I was about to tell her we'd try to look up the information on the Internet, she whipped a small leatherette-bound book out with a triumphant flourish. Zabel and I both copied the information into our phones.

As we made our way to the door, Rhoda gave us an intense look. "Do you think that Great-Uncle Alastair's death had something to do with this letter he wrote?"

I wasn't sure how to respond, but Zabel wasn't at a loss for words. "It's too early to know for sure. We're just curious and we need to follow up on a lead."

"I wonder..." Rhoda folded her arms. "He was the sort of man who got obsessed with little things. If he was wondering about that movie, he wouldn't stop until he'd exhausted every opportunity he could find. So many times, I knew he was wondering about something, like some question about Sir Arthur Conan Doyle's life, and he'd miss doctor's appointments because he was at the library researching it. Once he was curious about something, he'd never let go until he'd got the answers he wanted."

Zabel smiled. "I understand. I'm exactly the same way."

CHAPTER SIX
The Alfriston Sherlock Holmes Society

Zabel and I sat in her car for several minutes, letting what we had just learned sink in for a bit. We were snapped out of our reflections by a rapping on the windshield. It was a woman who I would have guessed was sixty-five, but if she had asked me to my face how old I thought she was, I would have said that she was forty-five, out of both politeness and a desire not to provoke her annoyance.

"Are you two all right in there?" she asked.

Zabel nodded. "Yes! Yes, we are."

"Are you lost?"

"No, we're just getting our thoughts together."

"I see. Do try to hurry it up a bit." With that, the lady walked away, casting a suspicious glance over her shoulder now and then. It wasn't until she was some distance away that I could see she was walking a pet on a leash. After staring at it for a few seconds, I realized she was walking a small white pig.

I pointed this out to Zabel, who didn't seem to appreciate the notability of this example of animal exercise. "The nerve of that woman," she scowled. "We weren't bothering her or anybody else. But from the way she was glaring at us, you would have thought the two of us were snogging in the back seat of this car half-naked in front of a parade of schoolchildren!"

I required a great deal of mental effort to drive this image from my mind. When I finally managed to escape the jumble of my fantasies that hadn't been this strong since adolescence, I felt disposed to be charitable. "I expect that the news is just getting around that an elderly man was murdered yesterday. Maybe she suspects we had something to do with it, as we're strangers, and they probably don't get many there."

"Hmm! She strikes me as the sort of woman who broke down into tears after the anti-social behaviour orders were discontinued, once she realized that she couldn't get her neighbors into trouble anymore every time their dogs made a mess on her lawn. She's probably going to do a circuit around the block, and if she sees us here again she's likely to report us for loitering." Zabel turned on her ignition and eased the car down the road, her lips clamped tightly together.

"Perhaps it's just as well we're getting out of here. My record's clean and I'd like it to stay that way."

"Good for you. Mine isn't."

"What? Were you in prison?"

"Oh, no. Not that. But I've gotten my share of fines and cautions. A couple of times I rummaged through rubbish bins looking for evidence on a potential suspect and got charged for littering, even though most of the garbage was scattered around the ground well before I got there. One woman charged me with intimidation when all I did was politely ask her why none of her last three ex-husbands has been seen in a year. Three times I've been cautioned for urban exploration."

"What's that?"

"It's when you poke around abandoned buildings and storm drains. Some people consider it a form of spelunking. I was looking for murder weapons and human remains. In two cases, the police officers understood, but they said I could get hurt if I wasn't careful. The third officer was royally cheesed off at me. I believe he thought I was implying the official investigators hadn't done enough to solve the case. Which I was, to be honest."

"That's not too bad."

"And once a M.P. wanted me arrested for assault."

"What's the story behind that one?"

"I was looking into an embezzlement charge. When I went to confront the M.P. after the forensic audit I'd had done, he laughed at me and his hands started wandering. So I blackened his eye and got out of there. Well, he raised merry hell about it, and I felt the heat for a bit because it was my word against his and you can't get fingerprints off of an ankle-length satin skirt, so I had no proof. Fortunately, one of the investigating officers was rather comely, and when he made a pass at her, she took my side before formal charges were filed."

Zabel sighed. "I've been wondering for a long time if I'm in the right line of business."

"You've got a huge social media following."

"They've changed the rules and my ad revenue money's plummeted. And you can't eat likes and shares. Without a proper media company behind me, I'm going to have to rethink my career strategy."

"Have you ever thought about writing a book?"

"I've tried, but I tend to run out of steam after two thousand words."

"A book of articles might work."

"I suppose so," she sighed. "Anyway, enough about my journalistic struggles. What say we track down the surviving members of the Alfriston Sherlock Holmes Society?"

I took Wren Bevan and she took Agrona Lowell. We both hunched over our mobiles for a couple of minutes, flatting our thumbs until we found what we needed. After a couple of calls, they both agreed to meet us at The Cheese and Bacon Pub for lunch. Given my personal gastronomic tastes, the establishment sounded promising.

When we arrived, the pub didn't *look* particularly encouraging, but its *smell* gave me cause for optimism. The Cheese and Bacon was one of those establishments whose clientele appear to be extremely light-sensitive. The frosted windows only provided a slight glow from the afternoon sun, and the bulbs in the lamps hanging from the ceiling appeared to be hanging on through an impressive last gasp of sheer willpower. After rubbing my knuckle on a wooden table, I learned that the establishment only appeared to be dusty, due to the dim light, but it was actually rather cleaner than it seemed.

Despite the dubiousness of the surroundings, an unquestionably wonderful array of odors was coming from behind a pair of doors off to the side.

The only other person we could see in the pub was behind the bar, a man who shaved his head bald, but as compensation, appeared to have never brought a razor to his chin in five years. He was slightly taller than he was wide, and he was so intent on his mobile that he didn't bother to greet us. I cleared my throat and received no response. Zabel walked up to him and greeted him with a "Hello" and a bright smile. That got his attention.

"Can we have a table for four, please?"

"Take your pick. It's a slow day."

"Can we see your lunch menu?"

"No menu. If you want food, you have the platter."

"The platter? What's that?"

"Meats.   Cheeses.   Bread and biscuits. Sometimes fruit and veg if they're not mouldy."

"No other options?"

"There's the vegetarian platter. It's the same as the regular platter, only without the meats. The price is the same."

"I see."

He raised an eyebrow. "You're not from around here, are you? Londoner?"

"Yes."

"Are you one of those vegans? The last Londoner who was here was a vegan. We can make you a special vegan platter."

"Is that the vegetarian platter without the cheese?"

"It's water biscuits and carrots, if the chef feels like peeling them."

"For the same price?"

"Of course. It's only fair. The cook risks losing a finger every time he peels one of those wretched things. Don't know why we keep them on the menu. They're dangerous. The price reflects the hazard."

"I see. I was just curious. I'll probably have the regular platter, though we'll have to wait until the rest of our party comes before we place the order."

"We're here. We'll have the regular platter for four, Bunko." We turned around and saw a man and a woman, both of mature years, standing behind us. The man, presumably Wren Bevan, wore a deerstalker hat and a brown Inverness cape. The woman, Agrona Lowell, wore the same, only in hunter green.

The bartender, or Bunko, as I shall now call him, nodded, swiveled his head ninety degrees to the left, and bellowed. "Platter! Four!"

"Got it!" a voice squeaked behind the kitchen door.

Returning his head to its standard position, Bunko asked, "What're you drinking?"

"I'll have a pint of ale," Mr. Bevan ordered.

"It's a bit early for a drink, isn't it?" Miss Lowell asked.

"You sound like my ex-wife. I want my ale."

"Fine." Miss Lowell sighed. "Lemon squash for me."

Zabel had the same as Miss Lowell, and I ordered a soda water with lime.

Bunko poured our drinks, and my concerns that he might shatter the glasses in his massive hands proved unfounded. Miss Lowell led us to a table by the window, shrugged out of her cape, and smiled at us.

"It's terrible about Alastair, but at least we can take comfort in the fact that he went exactly the way he wanted to go."

"He was smothered in a library."

"Exactly! It was his dearest wish to be involved in a real-life murder mystery. He would have preferred to be the detective, but I'm sure he would settle for the role of victim. Not that he had any choice in the matter."

I wandered into the relative comfort of my personal thoughts, and wondered which I would prefer– a quiet, anonymous natural death in my bed, or lasting fame from being the victim of one of the most celebrated murder cases of the century. I decided on the former. There's nothing particularly appealing about everybody thinking about you as a victim.

"Do you have any thoughts on who might have done it?" Zabel asked.

Miss Lowell shot Zabel a very shrewd glance. "Well, I have no doubt that you've put together a very nice little list of suspects. When you called me, you said that you met Alastair's great-niece. Nice girl, not a killer, but you'd remiss if you didn't put her on your list. Now her husband. Have you met him?"

"No."

"I don't care for him. Shady like the base of a tree facing the sun."

Mr. Bevan cleared his throat disapprovingly. "If the sun was shining on the base of the tree, the shadow would be on the *other* side of tree."

"You're wrong."

"No, I'm not."

"This past summer I sat against the trunk of a tree in my yard, facing the sun so I had better reading light. It was shady and cool and very pleasant."

"I think I know the tree you're talking about. The tall one?"

"They're *all* tall."

"Not the one by the front fence. The one I'm thinking of has huge branches and thick leaves. You'd get shade from that."

"You see? I was right!"

"No, you weren't. Because *I* was talking about the shadow of the actual tree, and most of it would be going in the opposite direction of the sun!"

"Oh, what do you know, you old fool!"

This went on for four minutes. Zabel and I couldn't stop it. We both tried to make peace between them, and we failed miserably. The chairs paid more attention to what we were saying than the surviving members of the Alfriston Sherlock Holmes Society. We managed to redirect the conversation only when Mr. Bevan downed the remains of his glass in one gulp, stood up, and told us he was sick of her and was heading home. A bit of undignified pleading and a reminder that we were trying to find out what had happened to their mutual friend managed to get him to sit back down, coupled with a promise to buy him another pint of ale.

"Are we on your list of suspects?" Mr. Bevan asked us. "You know we're set to inherit his collection of Sherlock Holmes memorabilia."

"Yes, and I don't know how we're going to decide who's going to get what," Miss Lowell added. "We both want the same things, which is to say, everything."

"One of us shall probably wind up murdering the other over the collection, but neither of us would have ever harmed poor Alastair, even for his wonderful collection," Mr. Bevan informed us."

"We could flip coins for items."

"Coin flips are easy to rig."

"What on earth are you raving about? I don't know how to make a coin turn up heads or tails."

"It's all in how you position it on your fingers. Anybody could do a little research and figure out how to tilt the odds in your favor. A little practice and you'd be getting sixty, sixty-five percent of the collection."

No one will fault me for skipping over the next minute of bickering. I only managed to restore peace by rushing back to Bunko, getting a fresh pint of ale, and setting it in front of Mr. Bevan. After lowering the level of the glass by twenty-five percent, he forgot why he was arguing with Miss Lowell.

"Perhaps we could ask a mediator to decide who gets what," Miss Lowell was unwise enough to remind him."

"Absolutely not. I was foolish enough to put my trust in a mediator during my divorce. Never again."

"You could do what one of my aunts by marriage did when her grandmother died," I said, kicking myself for getting involved. "There were about twenty family heirlooms that she and all three of her sisters wanted. So they wrote the names of the items on some little marbles and played Hungry Hungry Hippos for them."

"Did that work?" Miss Lowell asked.

"Well, one sister got nine marbles and another got only three. I hear that the two of them haven't spoken since, but actually they hadn't talked for four years previously after one ran off with the other's fiancé. I can't remember which one did that."

"But the problem with that is there's no guarantee that the collection will be divided equally," Mr. Bevan noted. "And even if we both get the same number of items, that doesn't mean that the value of what we get will be equal."

"We shall have to call an appraiser."

"Do you know anybody who specializes in Sherlock Holmes memorabilia?"

"Actually, I do," I answered, hating myself even more for getting involved. "I bought some stuff from him when I was decorating my office." I managed to dig his number out of my mobile, and with a Herculean effort, Zabel managed to redirect the conversation back to the murder.

"We discovered that your late friend was obsessed with a long-lost Sherlock Holmes television production."

"That was just like Alastair," Miss Lowell laughed. "He'd be thinking about some lost silent film or missing radio broadcasts from the

Rathbone/Bruce era, and he'd spend weeks trying to dig up information on them. He'd skip meals and refuse to go to bed sometimes until he found what he was looking for. And when he finally gave something up as a bad job two whole months or more would have passed."

"You're talking about *The Diamond Deerstalker*, right?" Mr. Bevan asked.

"*Deadly Deerstalker*," I corrected.

"That's right. I was stunned when he told me about it. I thought I'd seen every Sherlock Holmes movie in existence, at least the ones that still exist. You know that some of the oldest movies have crumbled into celluloid dust decades ago, right?" I told him I did. "Funny, I don't remember anything about it, although I didn't really get interested in Sherlock Holmes until the 1970s. I was never much of a reader growing up, but my son was a fan, and he asked me to read the stories to him, and I was hooked." Mr. Bevan launched into a monologue about how his son was the only good thing to come out of his marriage, and we couldn't get him to pause until Bunko sauntered up to our table and slapped down a square platter that covered the entire table. Luckily, Zabel and I managed to snatch our drinks away before they were crushed by the massive spread.

"This is what you'll be eating," Bunko informed us, pointing as he spoke. "Meats. Bacon. Very crispy. Not burnt. All the extra grease has been sponged off with paper towels. Hamburger steaks. Chicken tenders. Scotch eggs. Sausage rolls. Bangers. Best pork. A little garlic in them. No nitrates, just natural pig from a local organic farm. Cheeses. Stilton. Barkham Blue. Cheshire. Red Windsor. Wensleydale. Parlick Gell. Tunworth. Oxford Isis. Renegade Monk. Coquetdale. Sage Derby. That's *sage*, I said. The green veins aren't mould. Edmund Tew. Hereford Hop. Lincolnshire Poacher. Appledore. I don't remember this last one, but it's good. The bread is fresh-baked from the neighborhood bakery, and we make our water crackers ourselves. Farm butter. Also apple slices. Egremont Russet and Royal Gala. They're organic, too. And finally, radishes from our garden. No carrots. You know why."

I previously mentioned that a wonderful smell was wafting out of the kitchen. It was ten times better in close proximity to the food. There's no other way to describe the scent of our lunch. In terms of

113

quantity, it wasn't so much a platter as a buffet. Not that I was complaining, but Miss Lowell seemed overwhelmed. "We should have just ordered the platter for one and shared."

"No splitting servings," Bunko informed us. "Anybody who eats from the platter pays full price, and the platter reflects the amount of people eating."

"How much does it cost per person?" I wondered.

"Twenty pounds. Gratuity not included but appreciated."

It was much more than I usually spent on a lunch. but given the portion size, it was a pretty good deal for a week's worth of hearty lunches.

"Don't worry," Mr. Bevan said as he helped himself to the bacon. "Anything we don't finish can be boxed up and taken home. I come here all the time, and I eat what's left for days afterwards."

"That makes sense, looking at your waistline," Miss Lowell snipped as she selected apples and radishes.

"Didn't your fiancé run away after he tasted the meal you made for him four decades ago? Wasn't it a salad that scared him off?"

The barbs were traded for another couple of minutes, and Zabel and I both felt so uncomfortable we just ate until they ran out of steam. Finally, Miss Lowell halved a radish with her front teeth and groaned, "I really think that the Alfriston Sherlock Holmes Society won't survive the loss of Alastair."

"How did you form the Society?" Zabel asked

"One day Alastair put a little notice up in the library asking if there were any fans of Sherlock Holmes who would be interested in getting together. We were the only ones who responded," Mr. Bevan explained. "We started having tea, sometimes meals together, talking about the stories. He tried to put out a newsletter, but neither of us are really much for writing, and it was mostly just him when he'd collect a few of his thoughts and theories once a year. Sometimes he'd print out a couple of dozen copies and put them in the library, and they'd sit there for a few weeks before the librarian started tossing them in the recycling bin two or three at a time to make him think that people were taking them."

"It didn't fool him," Miss Lowell noted. "He learned a few things from reading Conan Doyle." I don't know how he figured out what the librarian was doing, but he knew what was happening. That's why he stopped printing it."

"Alastair was the glue that held the Society together," Mr. Bevan noted. "You may have noticed that the two of us don't get along that well. I rather think that this lunch will be the last get-together we have. The Society will be disbanded after this afternoon."

"The Society won't be officially disbanded until after we divide the inheritance," Miss Lowell corrected. "Still, I'd rather our friend was still alive. Alastair was my friend and his friend, even if the two of us aren't really chums."

I suddenly remembered an earlier question that hadn't been properly answered, and I stuck my oar in before they could start squabbling again. "So... do you remember anything Alastair said about *The Deadly Deerstalker*?"

"Only that he was trying to track down the people involved," Miss Lowell shrugged. "I know he found this article that mentioned the actors who played Holmes and Watson, and the director, too. But two of them were dead, and I can't remember which ones."

"The actor who played Watson and the director died ages ago, I believe," Mr. Bevan noted. "It's the actor who played Holmes who's still alive."

"Declan LeCeil?" Zabel asked, displaying an impressive memory.

"That sounds vaguely correct. I believe Alastair tracked him down to some nursing home outside London. The Peaceful Countryside Retirement Home." Alastair was trying to get in touch with him, but the Home won't direct your phone calls unless you're on a list, and LeCeil didn't respond to his letter."

Zabel worked her magic on her mobile. "Peaceful Countryside Retirement Home. That's right on the way back home. If we'd taken a different route, we would've passed it on the way here."

How it started I couldn't say, but either Miss Lowell or Mr. Bevan made some remark about the last recent adaptation of a Sherlock Holmes story that they'd all seen together, and it didn't take long before it was clear that the two of them had very different opinions about that production. Neither was afraid to say exactly what they were thinking, and their disagreement turned personal amazingly quickly. Zabel and I tried to pour oil on the turbulent waters, but we would've needed the entire Exxon Valdez to have had any impact. Finally, Miss Lowell threw down her napkin and flounced out of the pub without another word. She didn't pay for her share of the lunch, but given the fact that she'd only taken about twenty-five pence worth of apples and radishes, I figured she wasn't exactly robbing us blind. I was a bit more upset when Mr. Bevan indicated that he believed that he was here as our guest, and therefore his wallet would remain securely in his pocket.

Zabel wasn't too upset at this presumption, and following her lead, I said goodbye to forty pounds plus a generous tip as we split the bill between the two of us. I would have felt better about it if Mr. Bevan had been able to tell us more useful information, but repeated trips to the well brought no additional water.

In any event, even after Mr. Bevan took a large paper bag filled with leftovers home, Zabel and I still had three bags worth of assorted foodstuffs, so I figured I hadn't come out a loser on the deal. I would have objected to Mr. Bevan taking food without paying, but he looked so happy I figured I could afford to be generous.

On our way to the Peaceful Countryside Retirement Home, I called ahead to ask about visiting Mr. LeCeil.

"We do not allow visitors without forty-eight hours prior notice, and all guests must be on the approved list," a very terse woman informed me before hanging up the phone.

A minute later, Zabel pulled the car over to the side of the road and tried to schedule an appointment for a tour, to see if the Home would be acceptable for her elderly grandmother. "We're not providing tours at this time," the terse lady replied, "We have a very long waiting list and we do not expect a vacancy to open up for at least three years." A very firm click ended the conversation before she could ask any further questions.

"So what do we do now?" I asked.

"We sneak in. It's not hard, I've managed to worm my way into care homes before, when I needed to interview people inside."

"How did you manage that?"

Zabel gave a very mischievous smile that thrilled me in a way I couldn't explain. "You'll see. There's a reason I told you to put the leftover food on the back seats and not the boot. There's no room in there."

CHAPTER SEVEN
The Peaceful Countryside Retirement Home

Zabel kept me entertained with stories about her previous investigations until we finally reached the Peaceful Countryside Retirement Home. It wasn't that aptly named. It was too close to the city to be considered the countryside, and from the various urban noises coming from all directions, it wasn't that peaceful, either. It was an ordinary-looking building surrounded by a fair amount of lawn space, and Zabel parked a short distance away from the main entrance and watched the building for a minute until she saw an employee walking outside.

"Standard dark blue nursing uniform. Perfect." Zabel hopped out of the car and hurried around to the boot. A tap of her key fob and it popped open to reveal a huge stack of neatly labelled garment bags. "I find it necessary to put on a disguise from time to time," she informed me matter-of-factly. After handing me a bag marked "Business Suit," another bag labelled "White Lab Coat," and another saying "Bag Lady," she took out "Nurse/Carer (Blue)."

After I dumped the other bags back in the boot, she gave me what I'm pretty sure was a wink and as she climbed back into the car, she said, "Now, stand over there and make sure no one else comes by while I change. And if you turn around, I'll know, and you're walking home."

I was a very good boy and kept my eyes firmly in the correct general direction until she tapped me on the shoulder. I turned around and saw she was now wearing a dark blue carer dress and white trainers, and her hair was tied back in a sensible ponytail.

"You really have done this before," I commented.

"Yep. I often need to change my outfit in order to get somewhere I'm not wanted. I have some fast-food worker uniforms, athletic wear, an evening gown, a business suit, and a few others. Most of them I picked up for a couple of quid in thrift shops. I alternate what I keep in my car, but I usually keep a carer outfit handy. People tend to respond well if they think you look out for the sick and elderly."

"So what's the plan? Will you just walk in the front door?"

"I don't think we can be quite that bold. However, they're probably cleaning up after lunch, and that might give us an opportunity."

We tried to walk towards the back of the building without looking suspicious, and even though I couldn't see myself, I had the sense I was failing miserably.

After making it around the side, we saw a few large skips, and a man wearing a uniform similar to Zabel's, only with trousers, was tossing a couple of overstuffed bin bags into it. Zabel and I glanced at each other, wondering if there was a way to slip by him without his noticing us, but much to my surprise, the fellow actually held the door open for us. We thanked him quietly and stepped inside the building, trying to act like we had every right to be in there.

In the relative privacy of a little alcove in the hall, we discussed how best to track down Declan LeCeil.

Zabel tapped her mobile until she found a picture of the actor online. He was a dignified-looking man with a halo of grizzled white hair and the nose of a Roman emperor. "Maybe we should check the common areas for him."

"Maybe. It's late afternoon, though."

"So?"

"It's nap time."

Zabel saw the justice in this. "You're right. Still, no guarantee that he isn't in the recreation center playing bingo or watching telly in the common room."

We decided to explore a little bit, and if anybody asked, I was a visitor who got lost and Zabel was showing me the way outside. It wasn't long until we came across a wall filled with locked mailboxes, each with a little glass window on the door. Each mailbox was labelled with a name. It didn't take long to find Mr. LeCeil's, as they were in alphabetical order.

"There's quite a bit of mail in here," Zabel noted. "One piece might have the room number on it—"

She was interrupted by a loud click, and as the door next to the mailboxes eased open, I jumped sideways and did my best to conceal myself behind an enormous potted plastic plant. Zabel stood her ground as a woman wearing a carer's dress like, hers, only in green, stepped out into the hall.

This employee squinted at Zabel suspiciously. "Hello. I haven't seen you here before."

Not missing a beat, Zabel slipped into an unidentifiable accent. "I temporary worker. Agency send me because regular employee missing."

"Really? Who are you substituting for? Everybody was there at our lunch meeting."

"I not know. I go where I'm told."

The employee started giving Zabel the once-over. "Where's your identification badge? You're supposed to have one on you at all times."

Zabel started stammering. "I... I not have one. I... I not know I need one. I... I am bad. I... I am sorry. Am I fired? Please... please do not send me back. Is not safe for me." I've never known how some women can cry on cue, but I respected Zabel for her mastery of this power. "Please... I cannot go back. The bad men, they... they...." As she devolved into sobs, the employee rushed up to her, and while she slipped a comforting arm around Zabel, I slipped into the mail room, shutting it as quietly as I could.

Two minutes passed, and as the room was fairly soundproof, I couldn't hear what was going on outside. A light tapping at the door made me jump, but when Zabel stuck her head inside, I felt proud that I could tell her I'd completed my mission.

"Any luck, Addy?"

"Declan LeCeil is in room 41. Should we bring him his mail?"

"Why not? Might as well save him a trip."

We found room 41 with no difficulty, and though at least half a dozen people passed by us, none of them paid us any notice. A knock on the door of room 41 provoked a booming "ENNN-TERRR!" I couldn't be sure, but I suspected that Mr. LeCeil had performed recently in a production of Neil Simon's *The Sunshine Boys*.

Even if I hadn't already known Mr. LeCeil's profession, I would have known it the second that I walked into the room. It was a fairly small bedsit, but every available inch was a museum of Mr. LeCeil's dramatic career. A row of clothes that were clearly stage costumes hung on a rack in one corner. There were so many framed posters and photographs that it was impossible to tell whether the walls were painted or wallpapered. The top right corner of the wall validated my theory when I saw a poster for a production of *The Sunshine Boys* from three years ago. Apparently, Mr. LeCeil had been in everything from Shakespeare to lavish musicals to farces to a turn in Agatha Christie's *The Mousetrap*.

"Come in! Come in!" Mr. LeCeil's voice was warm and welcoming. He picked up a pair of glasses that were nearly an inch thick and placed them upon his ears and nose. "Do I know you? Have you worked here long?"

"No, I haven't," Zabel replied, not bothering to adopt her accent from earlier. "My name is Zabel," she told him as she walked up to him.

"You're not really a carer, are you?"

Zabel flinched. "What makes you say that?"

"All the nurses who work here use this powerful soap you can smell from Wales. They make them scrub themselves with it so they don't spread diseases. You don't have that scent. Also the tone of your voice is all wrong. The regular carers always talk loudly and slowly to us. If you'd been an actual employee here, you would have told me "MY... NAME... IS.... ZAY... BELLE!" Lovely name, by the way, my dear."

We were both impressed. "That's pretty good reasoning," I told him.

"Well, my eyes are good for garbage these days. On my good days, I can just see my memories on the walls. The rest of the time, it's all a blur. The glasses help, but most of the time, I just have to rely on my senses of smell and hearing. Speaking of which–" He pointed at the little table next to him, where an MP3 player and a speaker that would have been top-of-the-line technology fifteen years ago were playing. "Would you please shut that off for me, young man?" I did. From the little bit of dialogue I heard, it was a radio play, and I wouldn't have been surprised if it was one featuring Mr. LeCeil. "Thank you, dear boy. What's your name?"

"I'm Addy."

"Delighted to meet you, just delighted. I say…" He turned back towards Zabel. "Zabel… I recognize that name and your voice. Are you that true crime podcaster?"

"Yes!"

"I was just listening to your show on the Kray Twins and their legacy a couple of weeks ago. Good stuff, that. I'll have to listen to more of it soon. I was wondering why you both came. I was hoping you were fans who just slipped in to meet me, but that was just wishful thinking, I suppose. I've never been pestered much by autograph hounds, and I don't see why that should change now that I'm retired." He sighed. "Ah, well. No point in wallowing. But what are you doing here? I don't think I can help you with a true crime case."

"Well actually, sir–"

"My dear, please don't call me "sir." I was never knighted. Sorry if I sounded bitter. It's another sore spot for me. My name is Declan."

Zabel smiled and summarized the entire situation. By the end of her monologue, Declan looked stunned. "Do you actually think that *The Deadly Deerstalker* had something to do with that poor man getting killed? And with you getting robbed, young fellow?"

"We can't be sure," I explained, "but it's a possibility and we have to look into it."

"*The Deadly Deerstalker...*" Declan mused. "I remember it well. It was going to be my big break. My first of many potential big breaks in a very long and not particularly illustrious or distinguished career."

"You've been in so many productions," Zabel looked around the room. "If you ask me, your career's gone pretty well."

"Be honest, my dear. Before today, had you ever heard of me?"

Zabel's embarrassed shrug was her answer.

Declan wasn't the least bit offended. "No need to apologize, my dear. Perhaps I owe my long career to my relative anonymity. You can't get typecast if no one remembers what you've played in the past. But if I believed that there was someone out to get me and sabotage my career– and let's face it, in my darker moments I do– then my experience with *The Deadly Deerstalker* would be Exhibit A."

"What happened?"

"Well, you know the basic story. I was just starting out in my career, and getting cast as Sherlock Holmes was supposed to be my big break. I thought I made a very good Holmes. I'm sure I could have connected to the fan base."

"Sometimes getting the role of a lifetime comes with consequences," I noted. "Basil Rathbone got tired of playing Holmes because after playing the great detective so often, casting directors couldn't see him as anybody else, so he lost out on tons of roles he really wanted. Benedict Cumberbatch became an international star after *Sherlock*, but then he had to put up with thousands of people who think it's a grand joke to pretend they can't get his name right."

"Perhaps that's true," Declan conceded. "Still, I can't help but feel that there was a major opportunity lost here. There was talk about how if *The Deadly Deerstalker* proved successful, they might do follow-ups, perhaps turn it into a regular series. Silas, who played Watson, was a delight to work with. We became very good friends during filming and we worked together another half-dozen times over the decades. The director, Gaspard, was another story. He was a micromanager. You'd perform a long speech, and he'd make you do another take just because your inflection on one little syllable was a tiny bit lower than how he wanted it. Or your face wasn't pointed in the right direction. Do you know how many times he told me my nose was too big? Not a very enjoyable collaboration."

"That must have been frustrating." Zabel sighed.

"It's all part of the job. You work with the people you're assigned, and you complain only to your closest friends and family members, or you wait until a decent interval after the annoyances die to tell the world how wretched they were. Anyway, the movie itself was no masterpiece. The script was hackneyed. The dialogue was pedestrian. And yet... I think it really could have been the start of something big. Silas and I made a brilliant team. If we'd gotten a decent writer and director, we could've had a classic series. But we'll never know now, will we? My wife invited all of our friends and family to come over to watch the movie on the telly, and once we learned it had been preempted, it was too late to tell people to stay home, so we just had a very awkward party of people standing around nibbling their hors d'oeuvres, watching the coverage of the sad news from America, and telling us they'd come back when they finally broadcast the show. And it never happened."

"Why not?" I asked. "It seems like such a massive waste of time and money to produce a movie and then never show it."

"Well, to be fair, my boy, it wasn't really that big a budget. It was put together on a shoestring. They didn't even build an entire set for 221B. Just a little corner of a room, shot with a single camera, and a door off to one side to show people coming and going. It wasn't even clear if it was set in the Victorian era or the present day. We were wearing nineteenth-century-style suits, but another character just wore a regular suit and tie he bought at Selfridge's a week earlier. But that's actually a reason why we thought we might have a chance. A dirt-cheap production with a moderate audience has a much better shot at continuing than an expensive show with the same audience, even a slightly bigger viewership."

I kept digging. "I totally understand the original pre-emption, but why didn't they ever broadcast the movie?"

"I don't know. We didn't have a champion on the BBC who was determined to give us a strong slot in the programming schedule. There was so much new programming being filmed, and Sherlock Holmes wasn't very fashionable then. I told my agent to call them every so often to remind them about it, but I don't know if he ever followed through. He had a lot of clients and I wasn't a high priority for him. A few months passed, they turned into years, and when I finally started looking into it myself, someone told me the only copy of the movie had been wiped."

"You mean deleted?" I asked.

"Yes. That seemed very odd to me. I can't understand why they did that. I know that the BBC had a habit of deleting most of what was sitting around the archives to make more space, but I couldn't believe that they'd destroy a movie without ever actually broadcasting it. That just seems very wasteful to me."

Zabel frowned thoughtfully. "Could there have been something in the broadcast that someone might not have wanted released?"

"What do you mean, my dear?"

"Could there have been some reference to some current event or past scandal in the script that someone wanted hushed up? I know that doesn't make much sense as it was a period piece, but you said yourself there were anachronisms in the costumes. Why not in the script?"

"Nothing I can recall, but it was the better part of a lifetime ago. Why don't you look on that shelf there?" He pointed to a tall bookcase in one corner. "All my old scripts are there. They're not in any order, so you'll have to do some digging."

As Zabel started working her way through the shelves, I kept asking questions. "Is there anybody who had a serious grudge against someone else on the set? Someone who hated someone else so much that they would go to extraordinary lengths to make sure that their work wasn't broadcast?"

"Not that I know of, although looking back at

my career, I often think that there must be some sort of curse on me or somebody out to get me."

"Why is that?"

"I've never had much trouble getting cast. I've worked continuously since I was twenty-one, which is a lot more than most people I know can say. But that big star-making role has always eluded me, even after I think I've gotten it. I'm cast as Sherlock Holmes. You'd think that would be the part that made me famous. But the movie's never broadcast, and then it's destroyed. On three occasions, I've been in a brilliant new play. Once I was the lead, twice I had a powerful supporting role. Somehow, I got overlooked for the awards in London, but we were planning to transfer to Broadway. Twice the funding fell through at the last moment and we never opened. The time I played the lead, we opened on Broadway to rave reviews. Then, the morning after opening night, the producer had a stroke and died, and there was some sort of legal problem with his estate, and all of his ex-wives and children started squabbling, and suddenly a judge put some sort of a hold on his money, and without the cash, we had to close before we'd put on enough shows to qualify for the Tonys. They said they'd try to find a new backer, but such an angel never materialized. Once I got cast in a supporting role in a historical war film. Wonderful part. Everybody said that I was a lock for a Supporting Actor Oscar, even though I was in only four scenes, and fifteen minutes of screen time. But the movie was three and a half hours, and the powers that be insisted that forty-five minutes be removed from it. All of my scenes hit the cutting room floor."

"That's awful luck," I sympathized.

"Thank you, dear boy. Most kind of you. What am I forgetting? Oh yes. A decade ago I was cast in this amazing crime show. Innovative. Razor-sharp dialogue. I had this outstanding part as the antagonist. The six scripts I received for the first series were the best I've ever read. We filmed all six episodes, but three days before the premiere, the star of the show was arrested after he was caught showing excessive affection to underage livestock. It was *Deadly Deerstalker* all over again. They yanked the show, and it was never aired. This one wasn't deleted, but it's sitting somewhere in the BBC archives collecting dust. And then, right before I retired, I was cast in the title role in a production of *King Lear* at the Globe."

"What happened?"

"The pandemic. We went into lockdown a week before opening night and the production was never staged. I was so frustrated I decided to pack it all in."

"That's so unfair. You just can't catch a break."

"Well, what's the use of wallowing, m'lad? I would have liked to have won a few major prizes or become a household name, but I've made a living through acting. I was married to the same wonderful woman for fifty-one years and had three mostly excellent children and nine grandchildren. I'm luckier than most." Declan sighed. "I would have liked to have some little part that caught the public's imagination. As it is, I'm one of those actors who everybody's seen at one point or another but no one remembers. You know, I would have liked a part in one of those Harry Potter pictures. Being cast in one of those films is a sure way to immortality to the younger generation. I've seen it happen to so many of my colleagues."

Here he started switching his voice back and forth. In a lower voice he said, "You know Sir Peregrine Highbrow, the actor, don't you?" Higher voice. "Nope. Never heard of him." Lower voice.

"Surely you must know him. His Hamlet is legendary. His Brutus is the stuff of legend. You can still hear the echoes of the cheers he got for his performance as Richard III at the Old Vic." Higher voice. "I don't go to the theater." Lower voice. "What about the movies and television? He's won nine BAFTA's, two Oscars, four Golden Globes, five Emmys, a Grammy, along with three Tonys and six Oliviers." Higher voice. "Doesn't ring a bell." Lower voice. "Sigh. He played Edelbert Humperdink in the Harry Potter movies." Higher voice. "Oh him! I know him! I love that guy!" Declan resumed his regular voice. "I auditioned for every one of those movies and never got a call back. I don't know. Maybe back when J.K. Rowling was waitressing, I went to her café and absent-mindedly forgot to leave her a tip, and she's been holding it against me ever since."

"Found it!" Zabel made us jump as she yanked a yellowed script from the shelf. "Do you mind if we read this?"

"By all means, my dear. I can't do any reading myself these days with my eyes, but I hope that you enjoy it. Just promise to bring it back, please. I want to keep my collection intact."

"We will, I promise. I'll make a copy and give it right back to–"

Zabel was cut off by the door opening, and an imposing-looking nurse strode into the room. "What are you doing here?" she barked. "You're not a member of the staff. Why are you wearing a carer's outfit?"

Slipping back into her unidentifiable foreign accent, Zabel explained, "I from agency. I told to substitute for–"

"I was told about you. We don't have anybody missing today, and even if we did, we don't use an agency. We have a rotating staff we can call upon to cover absences."

Zabel didn't give up. "Oh, no. I think I go to the wrong nursing home. I make mistake."

The nurse snorted and a bit of something nasty shot out of one nostril and landed on the carpet. "You certainly did make a mistake. What agency do you work for? I want to call them."

"I no can pronounce agency name, but I have number on a card in my coat. I get it."

The imposing nurse advanced on Zabel. "What's your name? What country are you from?"

I tried to jump in and help. With a gasp, I informed the nurse, "You can't just ask people where they're from! I had a training course at work where they specifically told us not to do that! It's insensitive and it can lead to lawsuits!"

"And you!" The nurse turned to me. "You don't have a visitor's badge! Who are you?"

"It's all right," Declan assured her. "They're friends of mine. They're paying me a much-needed visit."

"This is not the time for visitors. You should be napping now. Will you get yourself into bed or will I have to drag you there myself?"

A mischievous little gleam glinted in Declan's eye. "You're in a hurry to get me into bed, aren't you? All these years and I still have an effect on younger women."

"Another word out of you and I'll have you cited for making improper comments, Mr. LeCeil!"

He shrugged. "I'll plead senility. They'll never punish me."

"You are incorrigible! Any more of that and you won't have any gelatin with dinner!"

"Oh, no!" A mock gasp and a smirk from Declan. "Does that mean no sponge bath either?"

"In bed now! And you two–" She turned a ferocious scowl on us. "If you don't leave the premises immediately I'll call the police!"

"You'd better head out," Declan sighed. "Please stay in touch."

"We will. Thank you, Declan." Zabel leaned over him and pecked him on the cheek, slipping a little piece of paper in his hand as she leaned over him. She'd confirm my suspicions later by telling me that she'd given him her contact information. The two of us made our way out of the room with as much dignity as we could muster, but as Zabel passed the nurse she looked her straight in the eyes and said, "I thought your performance in *One Flew Over the Cuckoo's Nest* was brilliant."

And with that, she stomped out of the room with me right behind her.

CHAPTER EIGHT
The Great Erasure

Zabel fumed for a while as we hurried out of the building, climbed back into her car, and drove away in the hope that we could get away before anybody followed us and took down her plate number and a description of her vehicle. I tried to start up a conversation a few times, but her terse response was that she hated officious people and she needed a little while to calm down. It wasn't until we passed the Connaught Hotel and I saw a familiar figure that the atmosphere in the car began to change for the better.

"Look over there," I pointed. "Isn't that Prescott?"

Zabel took her eyes off the road a little longer than was advisable and confirmed my identification. "It is indeed." Prescott was wearing the same expensive suit he had been sporting when we met him, but now it appeared a bit worse for wear. The jacket was split up the back, his knee was sticking out through one hole in the trousers, and the left sleeve was literally hanging by a thread. "I hope he has a good tailor," I noted.

"Look, he's dragging four big suitcases. His wife must've told him to pack his things."

"More likely, she packed his belongings for him and left them on the doorstep. If he'd been able to go inside, he would've been able to change his suit. Assuming, of course, that the damage was done before he got to his home. Or at least one of his homes. I'm guessing that both wives know about him now, which is why he's checking into a hotel."

"Which of the three women in his life do you think did that to him?"

"I couldn't say. For all we know, it was someone else. Perhaps one of his mothers- or fathers-in law."

"Yeah, that's possible. Think they made a fuss at his workplace and got him fired?"

"No. If he'd been terminated from his job, he'd be checking into a cheaper hotel."

"Good point."

I looked at her widening grin. "You're pleased about this."

"I hate cheaters. I've dealt with more than my share of boyfriends who think they're entitled to every woman they meet."

"Any guy who cheats on you is an idiot," I blurted out.

"Thank you." She placed a hand on my shoulder and my heart squealed with pure unadulterated joy.

I was too busy getting a grip on my pulse to say much more for a bit. By the time we arrived back at my flat, and Zabel had changed back into her original outfit, I was calm enough to join her on the sofa while we started reading the script for *The Deadly Deerstalker* together.

It was not a particularly enjoyable reading experience. The screenplay appeared to have been written by someone who'd watched a couple of episodes of a cop show and decided that he now had enough training to start work as a writer. The dialogue was rather flat, and the mystery was full of clichés and tropes that have been done a thousand times in the past. Of course, maybe they hadn't been done nearly so much in the early 1960s, but still, it was a disappointment from start to finish. Poor as it was, I didn't think that anybody would want to go to any great lengths to keep it from being aired.

After we finished the script, Zabel and I looked at each other. "Well, I don't think I'd pay money to see that," she commented.

"I think that Declan could have pulled off a memorable performance through sheer style and charisma, but the person who wrote this– Lysander Carew– needs to take screenwriting lessons."

Nodding, Zabel pulled out her mobile. "I wonder if he wrote anything else..." After a few seconds of searching, she declared, "It doesn't look like it. No writing credits at all, although he's credited with a few bit-part acting roles. "Man at Party," "Student #1," and "Concertgoer." I'd be surprised if those three credited roles had more than twenty words of dialogue between them."

"Maybe we should interview him," I suggested. "Assuming he's still alive."

"He has absolutely no film or television credits since 1963."

"Maybe he focused on the stage or left the business." I grabbed my mobile and started searching for "Lysander Carew" alongside Zabel. After ignoring the suggestion that I was really looking for an "Alexander Carey," I found a whole lot of nothing at first, but then we both discovered a link to a scan of an old newspaper article at almost exactly the same time.

Dated 1 November 1963, the article read as follows:

YOUNG ACTOR/SCREENWRITER FEARED DROWNED

The disappearance of Lysander Carew, 24, is now being treated as a likely drowning. Carew, a budding television actor, recently had his first television screenplay filmed for the BBC, and the production is scheduled to air later this month. Carew has been missing for several days, ever since the night of October 27th, when he went out drinking with friends. These friends said that an inebriated Carew declared his intention to go swimming late that evening, though they assumed that he was joking until they realized he had left the group. Shortly afterwards, they heard a splash a short distance away. Carew's coat and shoes were found at the edge of the Thames. Authorities are treating this as a tragic alcohol-fueled accident, even though Carew's body has not been found. As of this writing, there are no plans to cancel the search.

We kept on trying to find any further news of Carew's death, but there was nothing. "I'm going to give a friend of mine at the General Register Office a call," Zabel told me. "Hello? Samantha? How's it going? Mm-hmm. Well, he doesn't deserve you. You're much too good for him. Oh, that sounds like fun. Well, the reason I called is that I'm hoping you can do me a tiny little favor. Could you please see if you could find the death certificate for a "Lysander Carew?" L-Y-S-A-N-D-E-R-Space-C-A-R-E-W. He might have died in November 1963, though his body might have been found a bit later. Probable cause of death: drowning. And it's possible that he was declared dead after the appropriate amount of time elapsed. O.K. Thanks. Yeah, the usual rates apply. Name the wine, and I'll buy you a bottle of it. Sounds good. Bye."

Zabel turned back to me. "My instincts are telling me that this missing screenwriter may have something to do with our case."

"What do you think happened? Somebody hated Carew so much that not only did they push him into the river to drown, but they made sure his screenplay never saw the light of day either?"

"I don't know. Why would somebody be so sensitive about the whole affair that they'd kill an old man who wanted to find out more about the movie? You'd think that after nearly sixty years, the grudge would have passed. Plus the killer would be too old to go about suffocating people. It doesn't make sense."

I leaned back and thought. "In theory the disappearance/presumed death of Carew might have nothing to do with the price of Stilton in Derbyshire. These random tragedies happen all the time. A young man got drunk and drowned. Then due to an unlucky series of events, his movie was filmed but never released, and was presumably destroyed. But if I were writing a book, Carew's death would be the key to everything."

"I agree. Of course, the theory that Carew was murdered might be totally wrong. What if he faked his death for some reason and went into hiding? Maybe when Alastair Nithercott starting digging around, he came close to exposing Carew to the world, so... I don't know. I'm letting my imagination run wild, and that's dangerous to the integrity of the investigation."

"Right.   There's another couple of big questions that pop up after reading the screenplay."

Zabel smiled. "Let me guess. How the heck did it get made?"

"Exactly. It's amateurish and the dialogue is stilted. Why would somebody decide to take a risk on an unknown screenwriter, especially one of questionable talent? It doesn't add up. Maybe he was blackmailing someone influential into producing the script."

"But he was also an actor, wasn't he? If he were blackmailing somebody, wouldn't he push to have himself cast in the lead role or something like that?"

"Fair point, Zabel. I just don't know. Maybe his acting was so poor no amount of blackmail juice could get him a role."

The sound of a key in the door startled us both, and a moment later Sanna bustled into the flat. She saw us the couch and smiled. "You two look cozy."

As my face reddened, Zabel laughed. "We've had a busy day."

"Can you give me three minutes to get out of this wretched suit and get comfortable? Then I want to hear everything you've been doing today." As

Sanna hurried to her room, she put her hand on my shoulder, leaned close to my ear, and then in a stage whisper loud enough to be heard in Glasgow, added "*Everything*, Addy."

Zabel chuckled. "By the way," she called out to Sanna. "We picked up dinner."

"Excellent!" declared Sanna from her room. "What did you get?"

"The Cheese and Bacon's lunch platter," I answered. "It's pretty great."

"The Cheese and Bacon?"

"We'll tell you the whole story at dinner."

Jasper burst out of his room on cue. "Did I hear 'cheese and bacon?'"

After answering in the affirmative, Zabel and I started taking out the leftovers. I reheated the various meats in a frying pan while Zabel set the cheese, bread, butter, crackers, apples, and radishes out on a couple of plates. By the time Sanna was back out in her sweats, we were just about ready to gather around our tiny little dining table.

Jasper was about to dive in headfirst before Zabel politely suggested he should wash his hands before eating. The way he stared at the soap dispenser by the kitchen sink, as if he'd never noticed it before now, discomforted me, and made me fear for the sanitary purity of all the surfaces in the flat he'd touched since he took up residence here.

After a few bites of a sandwich she'd made with three different kinds of meat and four different kinds of cheese, Sanna expressed her appreciation. "This is great! Where'd you get this again?"

"We'd better start from the beginning," I explained. Zabel and I started telling the story of our day, switching back and forth so one could talk while the other ate. Jasper and Sanna both seemed absorbed by both the narrative and the meal, because neither said a word until we were caught up to the present moment.

Shortly before we reached the point in the narrative where the nurse had shooed us out of Declan's room, Zabel's mobile rang and she excused herself from the table. By the time she returned, I had just wrapped up the story. "That was my friend from the General Register Office," Zabel explained. "She's checked the records, and as far as she can tell, Lysander Carew's body was never found. He was declared dead in 1971, when his sister wanted to get his share of an inheritance left to them by their parents. She died in 2005, by the way, never married, no children."

"So there was never any conclusive evidence of Cashew's death?" Sanna asked.

"Carew. No."

"Then there's a chance that an eighty-plus-old man is out there somewhere after faking his death for some reason?"

"Yes," I agreed. "Or, conversely, there's also a fair chance that his dead body has been rotting at the bottom of the Thames or in a shallow grave in the countryside for over six decades."

"I don't understand why the BBC destroyed the only copy of *The Deadly Deerstalker*," Sanna noted. "It's very suspicious."

After Zabel and I agreed, Jasper looked up from his sixth helping of assorted meat and cheese and said, "Not really. It makes perfect sense, given their policy at the time."

"What do you mean?" Zabel asked.

"You've heard of 'The Great Erasure,' right? Or 'The Big Deletion?' Different people in the fandoms call it various names. I've brought it up a bunch of times on my YouTube channels. Have you seen my work?"

"No, I haven't. Sorry."

"No need to apologize. You just met me this morning and you've been busy all day. But if you ever want to see videos about popular culture and major entertainment franchises, you should check out my channels. I livestream four to six hours a day, plus I also make a couple of additional videos every day–"

"Which is why you have no time for an actual job," Sanna quipped.

"I make enough for the rent, don't I?"

"How?" Sanna asked. "I know you've mentioned it, but I don't see how that's possible."

"I make a substantial amount off of advertisement revenue, and the rest comes from my Patreon account."

"Patreon?"

"My fans and supporters subscribe and send me money in order to support the channels."

"You mean there are people who actually pay you to hear you complain about the last season of *Game of Thrones*?"

"Yes. You know this, Sanna, I've explained it before."

"It's just that it seems so impossible to me that my memory can't maintain a grip on it for more than a few minutes. My logical processes tell me that it's inconceivable, so I forget it within moments of hearing it, thinking it must be some silly delusion."

"It's not. I have a similar business plan," Zabel explained. "At least until I get hired by a reputable news outlet, or I finally write the books people tell me to write."

"Getting back to 'The Great Erasure...'" I prompted Jasper.

"Right. We don't realize it today, but during the middle of the century, a lot of television was seen as an ephemeral medium. The BBC would air a program, it would be repeated a little later, and that would be it. People figured it would never be broadcast again."

"Didn't some people want to catch shows they missed?" I asked.

"At the time, the general attitude was, "if you've missed it, you've missed it." Television was considered an inferior medium, and people in charge didn't feel like catering to people who'd had to go out to a family dinner and had to skip an episode of their favorite program. And this was before the days of

VCRs and DVD-Rs and TiVos and video-on-demand. The only way to record something on the telly was if you had a small video camera of your own, and you pointed it at the telly when the show you wanted to record was broadcasting, and make sure no background noise got recorded as well."

"That seems inconvenient." Sanna noted.

"That's because it was. But the powers that be didn't care, because they thought that television programming ought to be treated like live theatre."

"Didn't they realize that good performances ought to be saved?" I asked.

"If you were working at the BBC at that time that was crazy talk. Video tape was just too darned valuable to waste by preserving a show for posterity, you see. There was no justification for saving a brilliant or hilarious performance, not when there was cheap tape to be had. Using a reel of video tape just once wasn't cost-effective, not when you could delete everything on it and rerecord something else on it, and repeat the process over and over again until the tape finally wore out to shreds. Coming from their perspective, not mine, the BBC wasn't acting like cultural vandals by erasing shows. They were being sensible guardians of the taxpayer-funded programming by destroying most of that taxpayer-funded programming soon after airing it."

"Didn't viewers ask to see certain programs again?" Zabel asked.

"Of course. Quite frequently. Sometimes their pleas for a rebroadcast were simply ignored, and on the occasions when viewer demand was simply too vociferous, they replicated the deleted show, by which I mean they had to reassemble the sets, gather up the original cast, and have them perform an encore of their production, which more often than not would be wiped clean from the video tape before you can say Jack Robinson. Truly, the accounting geniuses at the BBC were saving the taxpayers' hard-earned pounds through their long-sighted and sensible policies."

Zabel looked a little incredulous. "Nobody considered that people might want to watch those productions again in the future?"

"Well, the idea of being able to keep television broadcasts was an innovation in itself. Back in the 1940s and 1950s, there were no tape recordings of television broadcasts. Productions were aired live, and there was nothing left behind after the show ended. Now all of a sudden, they had these massive rolls of video tape– not compact reels or VHS cassettes, incidentally– and in all fairness, they took up a lot of space. The reels were pretty big and heavy, and as they started piling up, they ran out of shelf space at a lightning fast clip and started stacking them in the halls and dressing rooms and anywhere else there was a free surface."

"And they didn't think to build a proper warehouse to hold everything?" I asked.

"Remember, the BBC was government-funded, which meant that there wasn't much initiative to run it like a profitable business. They had enough money to keep producing new content, but they didn't have an economic plan to support preservation. Today, when someone makes a movie or an episode of a TV series, it's considered an investment with the potential to make money for decades. After its initial airing, people make money from syndication, DVD and Blu-Ray sales (though not so much these days), and licensing to streaming services. A TV movie has the potential to be a steady source of income for decades, properly handled, it could bring a studio money until the copyright ran out, which these days can last for the better part of a century, maybe even longer if corporations like

Disney keep persuading the government to extend copyrights to keep Mickey Mouse out of the public domain."

Jasper was really passionate about this subject. Only a subject that fascinated him could keep him away from the food on his plate. "But like I said, in the 1960s, the BBC didn't have a long-term investment mentality. They had a Buddhist mandala mentality. You know what that is?"

I did. "It's a complicated piece of artwork, usually consisting of a tabletop-sized pattern, made of colored sand. It can take several days to complete, and Buddhist monks design them as a spiritual exercise. After it's completed, it can be displayed for a short while, and then it's ceremonially disassembled and the sand is usually cast into running water. It's meant to emphasize both impermanence and the release of positivity into the universe."

"Right. Like mandalas or ice sculptures, people who made television during the 1960s at the BBC did so knowing that their art was planned to be ephemeral. Of course, not everybody wanted their hard work to be zapped by electromagnets two weeks after completing it. Some famous comedians wanted to use their own money to preserve their work, but the BBC was all, "Nope! Everything gets destroyed!" This is where it gets weird. It moved from the routine wiping of tape as an economic and space-saving measure, to an attitude where everything *must* be obliterated. The BBC did find that they could make a little extra money by sending copies of various productions out to other countries for airing there, but they were a trifle peculiar about it. They said that after the agreed-upon number of airings, the overseas markets had to either send the tapes back or toss them in a furnace. 'Burn or return' was the policy, and if a station in, say, Kenya, incinerated the tapes, they had to provide documentary evidence of the destruction. I know the reasoning was looking out for intellectual property, but honestly, when you think about it, the whole situation sounds like the BBC was saying 'We don't want it, and we won't let you have it either.'"

"But wait a minute. If the BBC wasn't in the habit of keeping old tapes, how come we still have all of *I Love Lucy* and *The Honeymooners* and so many other series?" Zabel asked.

"Those are American shows. In the States, they had a much more protective attitude towards their work, plus, there are so many different television affiliates and stations around the country, it was a lot easier to save shows as there were so many copies. So while the Brits were busily obliterating our taxpayer-funded popular culture heritage, the Yanks made darned sure that nobody laid a finger on *The Beverly Hillbillies.*"

"But wait a minute," Sanna frowned. "There are still a lot of shows from the sixties in existence."

"Uh-huh. But those shows either beat the odds, or the staff was slacking. This is just a theory, but imagine a big stack of tape recordings. If you needed to record something, you'd take the top reel of film off the stack, wipe it clean with the magnetic machine, record your new show, broadcast it, and then return it to the stack. The same wheel might be wiped and reused dozens of times, but the video tape at the bottom of the stack wasn't touched. So some tapes were lucky and weren't cleared out, and in other cases, the foreign networks that broadcast BBC productions said 'the heck with it' and said, 'Sure, we burnt your film,' when in truth they kept it safe and snug in a basement somewhere. And often, the BBC employees just didn't get around to reducing the recordings that were sent back to them to ash. Again, it's not clear why they were both so concerned about reusing tapes, but also obsessed with cremating tapes as well. Sometimes people who worked for the BBC took matters into their own hands and brought their favorite recordings home with them without permission. I'm not sure how that worked, because like I said, those things were big and heavy, so it's not like it was subtle and easy to tuck a wheel of film under your jumper and say you had a big lunch.

But if you're a *Doctor Who* fan, like me, you're both grateful that so many episodes survived, and furious that the BBC deleted most of the early seasons. Thankfully, what with all the situations I mentioned a minute ago, a lot of episodes survived. Unfortunately, fans are still hoping against hope that several dozen missing episodes will be found somewhere, somehow. Same with fans of a lot of other series of that era. The first series of *The Avengers*– the British spy series with John Steed, not the Marvel superheroes– has been wiped out and taped over, and fans continue to mourn."

"Does the BBC take a lot of criticism for its erase-first-and-ask-questions-later policies?" I wondered.

"Definitely. Especially from guys like me. If you're not aware of this situation, it's amazing how radically the business paradigm has changed over the last couple of generations. Defenders of the old policy keep saying 'We didn't know! We were doing the smart thing at the time! Why bother saving inferior work?' But if you ask me, it was a short-sighted and wasteful strategy that obliterated long-term financial benefits and audience goodwill in favor of short-term budgetary concerns."

"So moving back to the case at hand, you don't think that it was unusual that *The Deadly Deerstalker* got erased before it ever aired?" Zabel asked.

"Well, yes and no. If it had been wiped a year or two after the initial airing, I'd say it was perfectly normal, even likely. The fact that it was *never* aired makes the whole situation a bit more suspicious, but there's nothing that couldn't be completely explained away. I mean, it could have been a simple bureaucratic snafu. The network might have planned to air it eventually, but they'd already set up the programming schedule for a few weeks. Then as time passed, with more new programming coming in and no vocal defender of the production demanding that it be given a release and a prime-time slot, it could have just been forgotten. I suppose that it could have been easily deleted by someone who just didn't know that it hadn't been broadcast. That's a reasonable, innocent explanation. It would still have been pretty wasteful, though. Even a low-budget short television movie would've cost a good packet of money, and if anybody had found out about it there might have been some sort of backlash. But if the script was as poor as you say, then the deletion could have been accepted or even encouraged as no great loss, possibly even as good riddance to bad rubbish. I'm surprised the producers of the film didn't raise more of a stink, though."

"That's right," Zabel said. "Declan said he asked about the film's release and never got a solid answer. But the producers, who had an even bigger stake in it, ought to have raised more questions. Who were the producers on the movie?"

"I don't remember. That article we read only mentioned the two leads and the director... wait a minute." I hurried over to the coffee table and retrieved the script. "Here we go. At the bottom of a cover page, it says, "A Mute Swans Production." Interesting name for a production company. It sounds like it should specialize in silent filmmakers."

"Mute Swans? I know them," Sanna informed us.

"Does your law firm work with them?" I asked.

"Yes. You know we cover a bunch of entertainment law cases and intellectual property disputes. We've got a few dozen production companies as clients, and I was just working on a case with them today."

"About what?"

"I probably shouldn't say too much about it because of confidentiality issues, but I can talk in generalities. Sometimes legal departments have to do a little digging to see if a company's rights to a property are ironclad. For example, let's say that the author of a book is going through a divorce, and there's a clause in the prenuptial agreement that says that in the event of the dissolution of the marriage, the wife gets half of the royalties of all works first published during their union. However, there are always problems when whoever worded the agreement didn't take all sorts of factors into account. What if the book was published in a different country first, before the wedding? Do the profits from film adaptations count, or just the book royalties? Bottom line, with a shoddy legal agreement, the film rights issue can be a total mess. That's where we come in. Theoretically, that is, because I'm providing an anonymous legal example here that does not necessary reflect real-life events. That should cover me," Sanna declared as she spread some pale yellow cheese on a water cracker and munched on it.

"So, after all that," Zabel mused, "we still don't have a definite reason why anybody would go to any lengths to kill Alastair Nithercott or Lysander Carew– or if Carew is actually dead. And we don't know if there's a reason why someone would want a television film buried or if it's all just some weird coincidence."

"That's right. For all we know, Nithercott's death had nothing to do with his investigation into what happened to *The Deadly Deerstalker*," Jasper noted.

"But then why the robbery of those letters?" I asked.

"Ooh! Here's a theory!" Sanna looked excited. "What if Carew faked his own death all those years ago? Reason to be determined. Then, Nithercott starts digging into the past, and Carew, or maybe his son or even grandson silences him because he wants to keep it covered up."

My head was starting to spin with all of the possibilities. "It's possible. Anything's possible. I just don't know. We've got enough information to theorize and not enough to come to conclusions."

We all talked and brainstormed for a bit until Jasper's eye fell on the clock and he announced "I've got a livestream chat coming up in five minutes! Thanks for the meal!" With that, he piled another serving of bacon, cheese, and bread onto his plate, and carried it to his room.

"I just thought of something," Sanna informed us. "My firm has a bunch of meetings with multiple production crews over the next few days, including Mute Swans. We're supposed to meet again at the end of the week, but let me email them. I think I can move our meeting to tomorrow morning. I think I could get you in with me, and maybe you could have the chance to talk to them. I'm sure I'm bending the rules a bit, but I don't care, so why should you?"

"Let's do it!" Zabel and I exclaimed at the same time.

Sanna called her contact at Mute Swans, and after a brief discussion, she was able to reschedule her appointment to ten the next morning. The three of us finalized our plans, and after a bit more conversation Zabel was on her way home. Sanna and I put the leftover food away. The meat was all gone, and there were only about three servings of cheese left. The bread, crackers, and apples were substantially depleted, but there was still an abundance of radishes. I wondered if they'd get eaten or not. Zabel had been the only one to have a full serving of them, Jasper hadn't so much as sniffed them, and Sanna and I had one each to make ourselves feel like we were being responsible adults by eating at least a little bit of fresh vegetables.

"So, did you crack and tell her you love her yet?" Sanna asked as she loaded the plates in the dishwasher.

"What? No! Why would you ask that?"

"Knowing you, it's a reasonable question, Addy. Holding back on your feelings is not one of your skills. I say that to help you, not hurt you."

"Thanks a bunch for your concern."

"Don't get snippy. I saw the way she looked at you during dinner."

"Oh?"

"She clearly likes you, and she respects you. I think you impressed her with your investigating skills."

"So… that's a good thing, right?"

"Don't get too excited, Addy. I think she's teetering right now between keeping you as a friend and going for a romantic relationship. Push her too soon, and she'll go for friendship because it's nice and safe and she's been burned a bunch of times before."

"How can you tell that?"

"It's written all over her face, but only other women can see it."

"So how do I know when it's the right time to tell her how I feel?"

"That's easy. I'll tell you."

"Sanna, if you know so much about relationships, why are you single?"

"The universe is conspiring against me."

We bantered a little while longer until the kitchen was cleaned. "What are your plans for the rest of the evening?" Sanna asked.

"I'm going to reread the script for *The Deadly Deerstalker* again and do a little Internet research."

"Well, don't stay up too late. You've got a busy day ahead of you tomorrow."

"I know." I didn't want to say it, but I was worried that I wouldn't be able get any sleep. I was just too excited.

CHAPTER NINE
Mute Swans Productions

As it turned out, I fell asleep on my bed halfway through reading *The Deadly Deerstalker* again, and by the time Sanna pounded on my door to tell me to wake up and get a move on, I'd gotten over ten solid hours of rest. Once again, Sanna pored through my closet and told me what to wear, informing me that if I planned on seeing Zabel more in the future, she'd have to take me to a respectable clothing store and update my wardrobe. I was too groggy to come up with a dignified retort.

Moments before Sanna and I were finally ready to go, Jasper answered a knock at the door in order to retrieve his breakfast pizza. "Heading out to investigate?" he asked through a mouthful of cheese and sausage.

"Yes. Want to join us?"

Jasper looked positively horrified at my invitation. "No, thank you! I have another group livestream in fifteen minutes."

"When was the last time you actually went out in the sunlight?" Sanna asked. "Because I'm pretty sure that you have not left the flat during the day since we all moved in here."

"I'm not a shut-in," Jasper growled, taking another defiant bite of his breakfast pizza.

"No, you just do a spot-on imitation of one. Do you even own a pair of trousers that aren't pajama bottoms?"

"I don't criticize *your* dressing style, do I?"

I made a few quick comments to restore peace in our household, and after taking a couple of buses, we saw Zabel standing outside the main entrance of the complex that housed Mute Swans' offices, waving at us.

After the standard social niceties, Zabel informed us that she was staying out of the way for a little bit while the authorities took care of a bit of a fracas in the corridor. "I don't know exactly what happened, only that they had a few prominent actors coming for negotiations over an upcoming production, and apparently a deranged fan approached one of the actors in the gents' in a state of disarray."

"Really? Do you–" I was cut off by the sight of a young woman with a familiar face being hustled out of the building by a pair of burly guards. She was wearing a long coat, and her hair was disheveled.

Sanna gasped at the same moment I recognized her. "I guess she didn't get the help she needed."

"Do you know her?" Zabel asked.

Nodding, Sanna explained, "I set her up with Addy a while back. I thought they might get along as they both like mysteries. Turns out, she was stalking one of the stars of–"

Sanna was interrupted by a shriek, as my onetime date broke free of the guards by bursting forward and wriggling out of her coat, revealing that though Zabel had described her as being in "a state of disarray," the phrase "a state of nature" would have been more appropriate. As she sprinted away in a zigzag pattern, she passed by us without so much as a flicker of acknowledgement or recognition.

Zabel blinked at the sight. "Is that a tattoo of Neil Dudgeon on her bum?"

"I can't be sure," I replied, "but given my knowledge of her background, I'd have to say 'yes.'"

Sanna's eyes lingered appreciatively. "The tattooist captured Mr. Dudgeon's eyes very well," she commented when I waved my hand to break her gaze.

It wasn't long before the streaker ran straight into the arms of a couple of police officers who happened to be passing by then. Once we were assured that they had the situation under control, we decided to head inside, while the sound of the newly captured woman wailing, "I love you, Neil!" rang in our ears.

"Here's the revised," Sanna informed us. "I'm supposed to go over some contracts with a few production companies this morning. Mute Swans is one of them. I can say you're here helping me with something, I'll be vague. I'll say I need to use the ladies', and that'll give you five minutes to ask some questions. If you need more time, cough twice and I'll make a face, say I must've had a bad kipper at breakfast, and then dash out again. Sound good?"

I was thinking that there was a fair chance that Sanna would ham up her expressions of discomfort, which could potentially spoil our investigation, but I knew better than to say anything about that to her.

"Who are we meeting with today?" I asked instead.

"Their names are Graysen and Rupert Fortescue. They'll want you to call them Gray and Rupert, but make sure you stress the second syllable. Ru-PERT, not ROO-pert. He's quite sensitive about that. They're the grandsons of the original founder of the company."

"I kind of fell asleep last night before doing any background research," I explained, making no attempt to hide my shame. "Is there anything I should know?"

"According to the research I did last night, Grandpa Fortescue passed away in the 1990s, and his son ran the business until about four years ago, when Daddy Fortescue retired to southern Spain with his third, much younger wife– or maybe she's just a girlfriend, I don't know– and left the family production company to his sons from an earlier relationship. Or relationships. They might be half-brothers. They don't look much alike," Sanna informed me. "They've produced a handful of light comedy series over the years, a few nature documentaries, but their stock in trade is wannabe prestige films about ordinary, working-class people dealing with run-of-the-mill domestic problems. Grandpa has cancer, Aunt Emily is a lesbian and her

174

parents don't approve, Cousin Joe is a heroin addict. That sort of thing."

"Are they any good?"

"They seem to average a 5.5 out of 10 on the Internet Movie Database. Nothing they've ever produced has ever won or been nominated for a BAFTA or an Emmy or any other major prize, despite being total awards bait."

By this point, we were in their offices, and the receptionist informed us that they'd be with us shortly. I looked around, seeing posters for television movies I'd seen advertised but had no desire to watch, as well as a mini-museum of props in plastic cases. I froze when I saw a rack of clothes in one corner. "Excuse me?" I asked the receptionist. "Are these costumes for a recent production or something?"

"Yeah. Not sure for what, though. Why do you ask?"

"No reason." I motioned Zabel and Sanna into a corner and started whispering to them. "Look. You see those two overcoats at the end of the rack?"

Zabel glanced over at the row of clothing. "The brown one and the grey one? What about them?"

"Those are the coats that the robbers wore two days ago. I'm sure of it."

Zabel took out her mobile and snapped a couple of pictures. "Well, well. I wonder what this means."

Sanna turned to the receptionist. "How long have those costumes been there?"

Shrugging, the receptionist replied, "Dunno. A couple of weeks? Maybe last Friday? Our costume people have been gathering up a bunch of items from vintage clothing shops recently for this new production their working on."

"What's it about?"

"No idea. The bosses talk about it sometimes, but it doesn't stick with me. They don't make the sort of shows I like to watch. I'm more of a reality TV person. I get a kick out of seeing rich, beautiful people behaving badly."

"Do you know anything about those coats there at the end?" Sanna asked.

"Nah. I haven't been paying attention to them. They're ugly clothes. I like my clothes with color, something that pops. These are London office drab, worn by grey faded people."

Sanna rejoined us and we conferenced in a corner. "That girl doesn't seem to know anything about those clothes."

"I agree, and she doesn't seem worried or evasive, which probably means she had nothing to do with it," Zabel deduced.

My attention was drawn to a framed photograph on the wall, with two mild-looking men with their arms around a very attractive model who had recently attempted to segue into acting, with unimpressive results. "Are those the Fortescue brothers?"

"Yes," Sanna said. "Why? You recognize them?"

I blocked out their faces from the noses down with my hands, and I recognized their eyes immediately, even if there'd been thick glasses in front of them when I'd first seen them. "I'm ninety percent positive it's them. They're the ones who broke into my office two days ago and stole the letters."

"That was a gutsy move, taking those coats and then putting them back here," Zabel mused.

"No guarantee they were going to use them in the show," I answered. "And besides, I don't watch their movies anyway."

"But they didn't know that."

"True enough. But why would the police look here, anyway?"

We were interrupted by the sound of the doors to the main office opening. A man in an immaculately tailored suit walked towards us. "Delighted to see you, Sanna—" As he looked up and caught my gaze, his face turned the color of milk. He started making choking noises, and just as I was about to step forward and give him the Heimlich Maneuver, he whirled around and hurried back into his office.

"Well that didn't look guilty at all," Sanna sniffed. "What are we going to do now?"

"I'm pretty sure that at this point we have a legal obligation to call the police," I said.

Zabel looked mutinous for a second, but after a few seconds of internal debate she nodded. I picked up my mobile, looked up Inspector Dankworth's number, and called. "I'm getting his voice mail... Inspector Dankworth? This is Addy Zhuang. Sherlock Holmes' secretary. I think I know who stole the letters and tied me up the other day. Their names are Graysen and Rupert Fortescue. They run the Mute Swans production company, and I think this is connected to the death of a Sherlock Holmes fan named Alastair Nithercott. I'm there now, if you want to meet me here. If you could get back to me as soon as possible, I'd appreciate it. Thank you."

"Which brother stepped out just now?" Zabel asked.

"Graysen," Sanna replied. "He—"

The other brother, presumably Rupert, stepped out of the office and turned to the receptionist. "This is a light day. Why don't you take a long lunch break, starting now? Come back around one?"

"Full pay?"

"Of course."

The receptionist didn't need to ask any more questions. She grabbed her coat and purse and sailed out without so much a backwards glance or a goodbye.

Rupert walked up to us. "Hello. Come on into our office, please."

All of my internal warning signals were blaring. There was something very odd in Rupert's face and in the tone of his voice. He looked nervous, but also a little aggressive. He reminded me of a mouse I once stumbled across in the basement of my building. I saw it scurry into a corner and squeak piteously. However, it also kind of assumed a defensive posture and arched its back, as if it were saying, "Please don't hurt me! But if you try to attack me, I will mess you up!" I decided not to take on that mouse, but I did ask the building's custodian to hire an exterminator. Rupert was acting a lot like that mouse, and I thought the way he was holding his left arm against his torso was very strange. I noted a slightly unnerving outline that was disturbing the natural lines of his tailored suit, and I did a little quick mental arithmetic.

While I was thinking, Sanna said, "Thank you, Rupert," and as she turned to me, I could tell that she was also noticing something was amiss. A glance at Zabel's face informed me that her instincts were also urging caution.

Leaning into Sanna's ear, I covered my mouth with my hand, and whispered, "Get behind him and pin his arms." Sanna gave me a little nod, and walked up to Rupert and gave him a friendly slap on the back before whirling him around and holding his arms in an iron grip.

By the time Rupert shouted, "What the hell are you doing?" I was reaching into his suit jacket, and in a pocket on his right-hand side, I found a gun.

Sanna and Zabel gasped as I pulled it out, but I knew as soon as I touched it that I wasn't holding a deadly weapon. "It's a fake. It's made out of rubber." It made sense. It's not that easy to get hold of a revolver in England these days, and lots of production companies have harmless replicas handy.

After a brief silence, Sanna burst out into raucous laughter. "Were you going to threaten us with a rubber gun, Rupert? Were you going to bluff us into standing still and getting tied up or something like that?"

Rupert struggled in her much stronger arms. "Release me! I want my lawyer!"

"I am your lawyer, Rupert. One of them, at least. Do you have a criminal lawyer on retainer, I wonder?"

This comment caused Rupert to pause and reflect. "Wait a minute. Does this mean that anything I tell you is confidential?"

"I'm actually not quite sure. As I don't specialize in criminal cases, and my friends here aren't lawyers and don't work for my firm, I'd advise you not to treat anything said here as secret."

"Then I say nothing." Rupert clamped his mouth shut with a touch of theatricality.

Before I had time to think of a way to persuade him to talk, Graysen burst out of the office. He saw me holding the rubber gun and groaned. "Oh, no. How did you know it was us who stole your letters?"

That shattered Rupert's silence. "Shut up! Be quiet, you complete fool!"

Graysen devolved into a quivering mass of stammering, twitching nerves. Little tears started forming in his eyes, and his knees began to quake. I kept waiting for him to crack and say something, but all we got was whimpering.

The thought flashed through my head that if someone else were to walk into the room and see me holding what looked like a firearm, there might be a certain level of unpleasantness that it might be difficult to clear up quickly. I slipped the rubber weapon behind an untidy pile of papers on the receptionist's desk. Neither of the Fortescue brothers noticed what I was doing, as Rupert had finally managed to break free of Sanna's grip and had his back to me, and he was shaking Graysen by the shoulders so fast that Graysen was incapable of seeing anything clearly.

"Should we do something?" Zabel asked.

"Nah, give him a little longer. He'll tire himself out soon enough."

Sanna's prediction proved worthy of Nostradamus, and it soon became clear that Rupert wasn't in the best physical condition, and he was rapidly losing strength in his arms. Another twenty seconds passed, and Rupert's grip weakened to the point where his brother slipped out of his hands and onto the floor. Turning around slowly, Rupert turned to us and from the enraged expression on his face, I was concerned that he was about to attack us.

These fears turned out to be unfounded, as Rupert took a long, deep breath, and said, "Do any you have an idea for a television show you'd like to pitch to me?"

None of us expected this. "I beg your pardon?" Zabel finally responded.

"I run a production company, and you certainly have an idea for something you'd like to see adapted for the screen. Everybody does. I can make this happen for you. All you have to do is tell me, and I can give you a producing credit. I'll have you working with one of the best screenwriters in the business. We'll get an awards budget set up, we'll find a great cast. With a little luck, we'll have the start of a beautiful business partnership starting soon."

"He's trying to bribe us," Sanna chuckled.

Zabel smiled. "I'd be almost tempted if sleazy producers with wandering hands didn't come up to me all the time, offering to give me my own true crime show. Thing is, I never work with anybody I can't trust. And I knew right away that none of them really wanted me in front of the camera. They wanted me in a completely different place, which was never going to happen."

"And I've seen the ratings for your production list, Rupert," Sanna added. "Your productions try their darnedest, but they don't have much in the way of viewership. That's a great suit you've got there, but it's the only one I've ever seen you wear. I've seen your car. I think you're just barely squeaking by. Anybody who works with you on a project would be lucky to make enough cash to buy a bag of day-old scones."

"So since you can't buy our silence, how about telling us what really happened with the robbery and the death of Alastair Nithercott?" I prompted.

Rupert opened his mouth, shut it, and then whirled around and bolted out the door as if he were being chased by a pack of rabid wolves. The three of us looked as each other, simultaneously asked if we should run after him, and decided against it, not out of laziness, but because we all instinctively realized that the now-bawling Graysen was the man we needed to turn to if we wanted information.

Sanna and I both took one of Graysen's shoulders, hoisted him up, and gently walked him over to a nearby sofa. As we set him down, Zabel poured some hot water from an electric kettle into a mug and added a tea bag. "Do you want creamer and sugar?" she asked. When Graysen didn't reply, she brought the plain tea over to him and tried to press it into his hands. Not wanting him to scald himself, she set the mug down upon a magazine on a nearby table, and the three of us pulled chairs up around him, effectively blocking off any potential escape routes.

Zabel pushed a few tissues into Graysen's hands. "You might as well talk to us."

Graysen whimpered a little more, but he seemed to have slightly better control of himself. He gestured towards the tea, and I handed it to him. He sipped a little, and when his hands still proved too floppy to grip the mug, I returned it to the table. "None of this was supposed to happen," he said.

"Of course it wasn't." Zabel put a comforting hand on his shoulder, and I found myself growing irrationally jealous of Graysen. "We know. We understand. At least, we understand a lot, but we need help with a few details. Why don't you start at the beginning?"

The tears kept coming from Graysen. "I haven't slept since it happened. We never meant to hurt that poor old man. And it wasn't me, anyway, but Rupert, he's not a killer. It was an accident."

"Tell us everything," Zabel stroked his shoulder. It seemed to have a soothing effect on him.

"It all started a couple of weeks ago. That's when the letters started."

"Who sent these letters?" Zabel asked.

"The old guy. Alastair What's-his-name."

"Nithercott."

"I guess so. He wanted to know about this movie my family made half a century ago. A Sherlock Holmes movie."

"*The Deadly Deerstalker.*"

"Uh-huh. I didn't know anything about it, and I thought I knew everything about every production my family's every made over the decades, even the ones where the recordings were wiped. When I was training myself to learn the business, I read every script we had on file. I looked at all of the production stills. There's a file on every production we've ever done in the company archives. And there was no file on *Deadly Deerstalker*. But there were... other notes."

"What do you mean?"

Graysen's face relaxed a little bit. "I've gotta say, it helps a lot to talk about this. It's the first time in days the knot in my stomach has been relaxing a bit."

"It's a wonderful feeling to get a load off your chest, isn't it?" Zabel's smile was warm and encouraging.

"Oh, it is! I tell you, I don't care if I go to prison or not. I just want my conscience to be clear! Where was I, by the way? I've forgotten."

From the look on Zabel's face, she'd lost the thread as well. After she turned to me for help, I promoted, saying, "No file on *Deadly Deerstalker*, but there were other notes."

"That's right. There was a little notebook from 1963, talking about this WWII home front drama they were panning. We wound up making it in 1965. It didn't do very well in the ratings. Anyway, there were a few comments about a Sherlock Holmes movie and the phrase "Deadly Deerstalker." It was clear that the project was actually being filmed, because there were comments like "Can we get the D.D. set designer to work with us again?" and things like that. I thought it was weird, because there's a file on every project Mute Swans has ever greenlighted, whether it actually gets made or not. But there was no file on *Deadly Deerstalker*, which I thought was odd, as we have all these one-page files containing notes from rejected pitch meetings. So I called my father. He lives in Spain..."

We waited a little while for him to continue, and eventually Zabel handed him the mug of tea in an attempt to get his tongue moving again. He sipped, and finally finished his sentence. "And when I finally got a hold of him– he has a very active social life, so there's often a gap between when I leave a message and when he gets back to me– he was very cross, and he told me that under no circumstances was I to ask any more questions about *Deadly Deerstalker*. He wouldn't say why, he just insisted. He screamed at me, and I promised I wouldn't write back to Mr. Nithercott. But over the next few days, Mr. Nithercott kept calling the offices, and sending more letters with more details about *Deadly Deerstalker* he'd found. Then somehow he found Father's phone number and started calling him, and this set Father off and he talked to Rupert. I wasn't allowed to participate in the conversation. Father often doesn't include me in certain situations. I don't want to talk about that."

"You don't have to," Zabel assured him.

"Thank you. You're very kind. Anyway, Rupert talked with Father, and when I spoke to my brother after the call was over, there wasn't one drop of blood in his face. Not one. Rupert's not a drinker, but after the call he took the bottle of Scotch we keep for guests and downed half of what was left. He's never done that before. It rather scared me, and he didn't answer my questions. Rupert was in a terrible mood all that night, and the next day, he told me that he had to take care of something and that I would have to take care of all of our meetings myself that day. Well, I agreed, figuring something was up but not knowing what. I thought he'd tell me once he was ready, but that evening he came back home– we share a flat, if I didn't mention it before– and he was drunk. He never drives after drinking, I was shocked. Anyway, I tried to ask him questions, and he threw an empty bottle at me and collapsed on his bed, still wearing his coat. I couldn't wake him, so I hurried down to the car and checked the GPS. It said he'd been to Alfriston. I'd never been there before, and I had no idea what he might've been doing there."

Graysen was getting the shakes again, so he tipped the remainder of the tea into his mouth, and I caught the mug just as it slipped out of his hands, saving it from smashing.

"After a few hours, I woke up when I heard Rupert stumbling into the loo. At least, he was trying to get there. I managed to get him out of his closet before he ruined all of his suits, and dragged him to the actual toilet just in the nick of time. While he was answering nature's call, he groaned, "I didn't mean to do it. I didn't want to hurt that old man." I asked him "What? What did you do?' But he didn't answer. While I was washing his hands for him, his legs gave out and I couldn't lift him, so he spent the rest of the night on the bathroom rug. The next morning, after he'd had four or five pots of coffee, I asked Rupert what he meant and what he'd done, and he grabbed me by the throat and told me to never mention it again. He spent some time on the phone with Father, but wouldn't let me hear anything. Then he cancelled all of our meetings that day, and told me that he needed my help, but I wasn't to ask any questions and I was to obey all of his orders without question. Well, we're supposed to be equal partners, but Rupert has always been the 'take-charge' type. We argued a little bit, and then he slapped me across the face and ordered me to do what he said. I'd never seen him like that. Then he calmed down, and told me that all we needed to do was retrieve a letter from a bank. He spent the next few hours working out a plan, and he took a couple of coats and hats from the wardrobe department, and some wigs and false noses and beards from our makeup collection, and we walked into your bank and... well, you know what happened next. You were there. Sorry about that."

"Quite all right," I replied. It was odd, but he seemed so apologetic and distraught that it was difficult to hold a grudge against the man.

"He took the letter, and two others that he said were decoys, and we hurried out of the bank. When we got home, I recognized the name "Alastair Nithercott" on one of them as he put them in a metal bowl and burned them, but he wouldn't answer any of my questions. Then the next afternoon I did an Internet search for "Alastair Nithercott" and saw an article saying he was dead and foul play was suspected, and Rupert went ballistic when I confronted him about it. So it's been very tense ever since, and I've–"

We were interrupted by the arrival of Inspector Dankworth and a couple of other police officers I didn't recognize. The Inspector looked as if he was in a particularly foul temper, and I found myself hoping that he wouldn't focus his ire on me.

"All right," Inspector Dankworth growled. "I want somebody to tell me everything that's been going on here."

An upset expression flashed across Graysen's face. "Oh, dear. Does this mean that I'll have to go through all of that again?"

CHAPTER TEN
Finally, Some Answers

We spent the next few hours answering questions and recounting the events of the two days multiple times. I have to give Inspector Dankworth credit. Every time I thought that he would burst some blood vessels and have a stroke, he brought himself back from the brink, and his face would shift from beet red to a shade more suitable for a healthy human being. I was glad of that, because he struck me as a decent fellow who was dedicated to his job, and I didn't want anything unpleasant to happen to him.

The Inspector asked me why I hadn't answered my mobile when he'd returned my call. I didn't have a ready answer for that, but when I checked my mobile, I realized I must have inadvertently silenced it after my call to him.

It was well past lunchtime and Zabel, Sanna, and I were finally back together in the same room, holding our stomachs and hoping that someone would think to bring us sandwiches. Fortunately, around the time people in Wales could hear our stomachs growling, Sanna remembered that she was a lawyer and started going around looking for people to inform that she was aware of our rights as citizens and demanded that we be allowed to leave. After five minutes of threats and pointed tones, Inspector Dankworth stumbled into the room and informed us that we were free to go, but to remain available to assist with their inquiries, please.

I got the sense that the Inspector was glad to see our backs, though I mumbled that I didn't want to miss what was going on with the case.

"Unless there's a car chase, nothing happens particularly fast in a criminal investigation," Sanna informed me. "Interviews take forever because solicitors are always telling their clients to keep their mouths closed, and by the time you're done waiting for the forensic tests, you'll have a full beard. Life's too short to wait around a police station. When they're ready to share, we'll know. Meanwhile, you should be worried about me. Cross your fingers and hope that I don't get chewed out by my bosses for losing them a client."

"That's right. I'd be surprised if Mute Swans survives this," Zabel noted.

"Do you think that Graysen was really as innocent, clueless, and uninformed as he let on?" I wondered. "He made it sound like he was completely in the dark about the death of Alastair Narracott, but I'm wondering if he was throwing his brother to the wolves."

"Leave that to the lawyers, Addy," Sanna assured me. "Either the brothers will team up and put on a united defense, or else they'll point the blame at each other and probably both go down in flames together."

We made our way out of the building and found our way to a kabob restaurant close by that serves enormous portions at prices so small I don't know how they stay in business. We ate and talked for a while, sharing our theories on the case.

"Just so we're all on the same page," Zabel asked us, "We do think that the Fortescue father or grandfather killed the screenwriter Lysander Carew, right?"

"I'd bet my chips on that," Sanna agreed, dipping the item in question in a blend of mustard and mayonnaise.

I concurred. "That's my theory, too. I think Daddy Fortescue is in this up to his eyeteeth and he recruited his son Rupert to hush up the investigation into *Deadly Deerstalker*. But... why? What was so bad about the film that he doesn't want anybody to even look at it?"

Sanna shrugged. "Don't know. I'm too tired to even think about it anymore. All I want to do is go home and take a nap." She froze with her kebab halfway to her mouth. "Oh, blast it. I have to get back to the office. There's still a few more hours in the work day. Maybe I should have stayed at the police station after all."

"Hey, you!" we heard the shop proprietor shouting. "What did I tell you? You can't stay here unless you're buying something!"

The proprietor was directing his ire on a very disheveled homeless man who was not-so-surreptitiously sneaking ketchup packets into his pockets. "Fine!" The homeless man barked. "I'll order a glass of water!"

Some obscenities were traded, and soon the proprietor screamed "Get out!" which provoked an indignant "With pleasure!"

As the homeless man strode out of the restaurant with a surprisingly enormous amount of dignity, I gestured to Zabel. "Do you recognize those trousers, Zabel?"

"I don't... wait a minute..." A moment later recognition flashed across her face.

"Will you watch my lunch for me, please, Sanna?" I asked as I raced out the door.

"Mine, too." Zabel was right behind me.

It didn't take long to catch up to the homeless man. "Excuse me, sir, but could you please tell me where you got those trousers?" I pointed to the pair he was wearing, which were dark green with a red plaid pattern on them.

"Nice, aren't they? I found them on a bush in the park. They're a bit loose on me, but for the price, who's complaining?"

"They're lovely. Here's the thing..." I quickly explained the situation with Rafferty Jarsdel III, and our new acquaintance was very accommodating.

"I see. Now, I'd love to help you, but a man in my situation would be grateful for a bit of a reward for locating these lost trousers."

Deciding not to point out that he was partly the reason why those trousers were "lost," I replied, "Of course! Just how big a reward were you thinking of, if I may ask?"

"Would ten pounds be considered a reasonable show of gratitude?"

"Absolutely!" I fumbled in my wallet and produced a note of the suggested denomination. I hadn't really thought ahead as to what would come next, so I was a bit shocked when he started removing the trousers right in front of us, in full view of the other pedestrians. Fortunately, he was wearing a ratty pair of blue sweats underneath, so no one was horrified.

As he started to turn and walk away, he suddenly spun around. "I say, I know we made a deal, but are you really interested in those ketchup packets?"

"What? Oh, no." I fished them out and handed them to him. With a tip of his tattered cap, the homeless man marched away, whistling a commercial jingle.

Suddenly remembering an additional detail, I called out to him, "Did you find a wallet?" In response, he sprinted away and disappeared behind a corner.

While the trousers were still in good condition, I noticed that there was a mild but distinct ripeness about them. "Think Jarsdell will still want these?"

"I'm sure any halfway decent dry cleaner will be able to fix the problem."

Sanna had some choice words for us when we returned, but she was placated by our quick recap. I asked the restaurant proprietor for a bag to carry the trousers, and after locating the nearest sink and giving my hands a proper scrub, I was able to finish my meal.

To be perfectly honest, I was rather disappointed with the events of the next couple of days. Up to that point, I'd been completely involved in the investigation, but that's the problem with turning a case over to the police. Once they get involved, they expect us mere civilians to sit quietly off to the side and wait for them to handle everything. I tried to get in touch with the Inspector, but he wasn't returning my calls, and there was nothing in the news about the case, but I wasn't sitting around my flat staring at the ceiling. As we finished our lunch and Sanna hurried back to work, my steely resolve finally broke, and I informed Zabel that I'd really enjoyed our time together, and I'd like to see more of her in the future, and that I thought she was the most amazing woman that I'd met in my life.

To my horror, I found that I was babbling and was unable to silence myself. Fortunately, Zabel knew how to solve the problem, and my fast-running mouth was quieted by the greatest kiss of my life.

Zabel and I spent much of the next two days working together, cobbling together a script for her upcoming video and companion podcast on our adventure, and revisiting a few of the locations we'd recently stopped by in order to take more photographs. We returned Rafferty's trousers to him, and he was quite grateful, though not grateful enough to reimburse us for the ten pounds we spent to reclaim them. We also spent a little time with Declan LeCeil, who regaled us with stories of his career and his many misadventures.

Around dinnertime two days after our fateful trip to Mute Swans Productions, and approximately three hundred calls, texts, and emails to Inspector Dankworth, we were finally honored with a reply, and he informed us that if we wanted to learn more about the case, he could stop by the flat that evening around eight.

I accepted his inviting himself over, though I couldn't help but ask why he was coming to us instead of asking us to visit the police station. "Because I know it'd be easier for me to leave your flat than it would to get you to leave the station," he responded. "When I'm tired of talking, I just can head home, instead of having to deal with four thousand questions from you." I couldn't argue with his logic.

Zabel were already in the process of making dinner, but there was plenty of Spaghetti Bolognese for the Inspector if he wanted to join us. The water was just starting to boil when Sanna came home. Kicking her shoes into a corner with vehemence, she groaned, "Don't get me wrong, I enjoyed helping you solve a mystery today, but when it comes at the cost of my having to stay late at work to finish my tasks, I think I might have to leave the detection to you two."

We brought her up to speed, and then we had to repeat ourselves one more time when Jasper wandered out of his room after a six-hour livestream discussion of *Batman: The Animated Series* with fellow YouTubers from five different countries. As his bedroom has its own bathroom next to it, he only leaves when he's hungry, and he has an innate ability to sense the exact minute when a meal is ready to eat, and he times his exit so he takes his seat just as the food hits the table and not a second earlier. It's uncanny.

Inspector Dankworth's timing wasn't quite as perfect. Zabel, Sanna and I were nearly finished with our meals (and Jasper was just starting on his third portion) when the Inspector arrived. I welcomed him inside, and he greeted me with a grunt that I chose to interpret as his way of saying, "Well hello, Addy! You're looking well this evening!"

Taking a seat at the table, the Inspector declined my offer of Spaghetti Bolognese ("Noodles are too squishy for me") and Zabel proffering the salad bowl produced a wrinkled nose and a wince of disgust. He did accept a glass of water.

"I'm giving you twenty minutes, and then I'm going to go home and watch a game."

"Which game?" Zabel asked.

"You're wasting time. Normally, I wouldn't be providing civilians with all of these details, but given your already prominent role in the case and the fact that you'd never stop pestering me for information anyway, I'm going to give you some details in the hopes that you'll leave me alone and not feel compelled to keep digging around and potentially cause some trouble for the case."

"Thoughtful of you," I remarked.

"All right, here's what we know. We found Rupert Fortescue right away. Once we had a description of his car and plate number, it wasn't long before we got a report of him heading north. We blocked the road, and he surrendered without incident. He asked for his solicitor, and that was the last word I've heard from him since. He has refused to answer any questions and nothing indicates that he will change his mind anytime soon."

"So you haven't learned anything from him?" Zabel looked disappointed.

"No, but his chatty brother is a different story." If I didn't know better, I could've sworn that the Inspector smiled for about a quarter of a second. "Graysen had the sense to hire a solicitor with a flair for plea bargains, and he's willing to plead guilty to stealing the letters in exchange for testifying against his brother and a suspended sentence."

"He's willing to turn on his own brother?" Sanna asked.

"They're actually half-brothers. Their father had an affair with Graysen's mother while he was married to Rupert's mother. No, wait. I think it's the other way round. I'm pretty sure about that, but maybe…. Anyway, what does it matter? Turns out, the brothers don't like each other much, but they've had to work together because dear old daddy wanted both his boys in the family business. With his brother going away for a while, Graysen will be producing movies all on his own from now on, so everything's going to work out just brilliantly for him."

"It sounds like you're not so sure Graysen's all that innocent of murder," Zabel noted.

"Well, in my business you get a sense of what people are capable of doing. Rupert's got a rotten streak in him, and I completely believe that he's capable of violence. As for Graysen, I think he's both weak and a sneak. Could he kill somebody himself? Doubt it. Might he stay back far enough to give himself plausible deniability while someone else does something illegal, and then profit when the other person goes off to prison? Wouldn't put it past him. Anyway, this leads into one of the reasons why I came to speak to you. Before the plea deal goes through, I need to get your approval as the victim. If you're willing to see one of the men who tied you up go free, then we can move forward."

"You mean you didn't come here just to see my lovely smiling face?" is what I wanted to say, but I realized right away that any smart remark would send the Inspector storming out the door, and as I desperately wanted to know what had happened, I hurriedly corrected myself and said, "Oh, absolutely. Forgive and forget and all that."

"Humph. You let go of a grudge a lot more easily than I do. Well, now that I know you're so forgiving, then I'll pass the message along. I should have said this earlier, but you all are sworn to secrecy on these details until everything's settled in court. That means no putting this in a video until I give you the green light. Is that understood?" He looked at Zabel, and she agreed, as did Sanna and I. The Inspector asked the same question of Jasper, and a few seconds later, after Jasper had swallowed a mouthful of pasta and concurred, the narrative proceeded.

"Well, then I guess I can reveal some of the Fortescue family secrets. I suppose I should go back to the beginning of the story, all the way back to the early 1960s. When Daddy Fortescue and his father were trying to break into the entertainment production business, they were hampered by the fact that they didn't have much money of their own. They were working as craftsmen for a studio, and they weren't making very much. So rather than shelving their dreams and settling for a mundane existence, they decided to find a faster and very illegal way of turning a profit."

"Robbing banks?" Jasper asked, wiping Bolognese sauce from his chin and nose.

"No. Drugs. The two of them started selling illegal substances to various people involved in the entertainment industry, but in a discreet way that kept their customers from knowing exactly who was providing the drugs. Pretty soon, they made enough to start their own production company, and a couple of short features later, they were up and running. But their rising stars hit a snag when one of their co-workers, a bit-part actor who did a bit of other work on sets, found out how they made their money, and decided to do a little blackmail."

"Lysander Carew," I said.

"Exactly. He'd written a script for a Sherlock Holmes movie, and no one wanted to touch it because it was a stinker. So once he saw the opportunity for a little extortion, he seized it. Mute Swans productions found themselves compelled to produce a television film they despised."

"I'm guessing that the blackmailer didn't know when to quit," Zabel said.

"He did not. He'd actually pushed to be cast as Holmes, but his acting talent was so dire that even he had to admit that he might be better off on the other side of the camera. Midway through filming, Carew told them about another script he was writing, and told them they'd better plan to film it next. Daddy and Grampy Fortescue were furious, because if their names were linked to Carew's terrible scripts, it would ruin their reputations and they'd never get the critical acclaim they desired. In case you're wondering, Graysen learned this from a deathbed confession from Grampy Fortescue, who died at the age of one hundred, after a lengthy if not particularly distinguished producing career."

"And Graysen's not in any trouble for withholding this information for so long?" I wondered.

"If it were up to me, he would be," the Inspector growled, "but apparently Grampy Fortescue's mental state was somewhere between "a bit spotty" on a good day to "essentially senile" at the worst of times. So his lawyer came up with the excuse that Graysen thought that his elderly grandfather was misremembering some old script that was pitched to him as something that really happened, so he ignored it. We can't prove otherwise at the moment, and I'm being politely but sternly told by certain powers that be not to dig around too much, not when we're being handed a statement that can wrap up two murders."

"Two? Then Carew was murdered?" I asked.

"Yes, he was. Graysen was pretty vague as to what happened, but according to Grampy's deathbed confession, Carew argued with Daddy over future blackmail projects during a break in filming *Deadly Deerstalker*. Apparently the argument turned violent, and Carew wound up dead. We're going to have to do a lot more investigating, but it was implied that Daddy Fortescue had to hide the body on-set, and when filming restarted a few minutes later, a bit of what remained of Carew was caught on-camera in one scene. No one caught it during production, but a little while later, when they were watching the finished project right before the air date, Daddy Fortescue saw the slip-up. Supposedly, it was subtle enough that a casual viewer might overlook it, but with thousands of viewers watching at home, someone was bound to notice, and might report it or raise questions. They couldn't re-edit it without raising suspicion from the director, who had no clue about what was going on, so they were panicking. When tragedy struck and the movie wasn't aired, it was the answer to their dark, twisted, murderous prayers. They made sure not to press for a new air date, and at the first opportunity, they somehow arranged to have the existing copies erased. And for nearly sixty years, it worked. Nobody asked any questions, nobody wondered why the movie hadn't been broadcast. Everything was fine until Alastair Nithercott started nosing around."

"Wait. What happened to Carew's body?" I asked.

"Ah. Thanks for reminding me. I forgot to mention that they faked the whole 'drowning in the Thames' thing in order to account for his disappearance, but they couldn't actually push the body in the river in case the body washed up somewhere and it was clear he hadn't drowned. The night of the murder, Daddy Fortescue rolled the body up in a rug or something and dragged it away to the old family farm. Apparently, before the Fortescues got into the entertainment business, they ran a little farm that grew decent apples but made no money. There was, however, a little pond on that property where some mute swans lived. That's where the company name came from, if you haven't already deduced that. So for over half a century, Carew's body has been resting at the bottom of an algae-filled pond. We sent a diver down there yesterday, and he found a skeleton without much trouble. The damage to the neck bones indicates strangulation."

"What's happening with Daddy Fortescue?" Sanna asked.

"He's legged it. He's transferred funds out of his bank account, left his much younger lady friend behind, and left sunny Spain, presumably for a country that doesn't have an extradition treaty. We're searching for him, but I don't know if he'll ever see the inside of the courtroom. It seems he's had four heart attacks over the past decade, and this added stress may bring on a fifth. He's a pretty old man, so I wouldn't be surprised if he's going to face a different kind of justice soon."

We were all silent for a moment, except for Jasper, who was still slurping away on a fourth helping. After a few moments, the Inspector continued. "Alastair Nithercott, as you might have guessed, was a pretty determined fellow and a skilled researcher. It turns out that Carew's sister kept some of her brother's old papers, and she donated them, as well as some other family journals, to an archive for future generations to study. Why they'd be of interest to anybody I don't know, but Nithercott tracked them down, and found Carew's diary. I guess the sister never bothered to read it for some reason. Perhaps she's like my mother. She found her father's journal after he died, but she could never bring herself to read more than a few pages of it. It was just too emotional an experience for her. In any case, there were a few oblique references to the Fortescues' drug business and how he blackmailed his way into getting his lousy script produced. Nithercott found them, and started asking more questions. We're piecing together the details, but one of Nithercott's neighbors saw Rupert visiting the house the afternoon Nithercott died, and told Rupert he should try the library. We won't know for sure what happened unless Rupert finally cracks and confesses, but my guess is that Rupert found Alastair at the library, begged him to drop the investigation, and Nithercott started to ask some very embarrassing questions. They probably talked for a bit, and Nithercott probably mentioned that he'd sent a letter to the bank asking if they knew anything about *Deadly Deerstalker*. The conversation probably turned into an argument, and when Nithercott started to get suspicious and raised his voice, Rupert put a hand or a scarf or something over his mouth to silence him. After a little struggle, Rupert realized to his horror that he'd accidentally smothered him. At least, that's a charitable interpretation–manslaughter. Maybe there was some level of premeditation, but you'd have to be pretty reckless to consider smothering an old man in a public library with witnesses in the next room."

The inspector stood up, groaning a bit as he straightened his back. "You can figure out the rest. Graysen claims his brother– half-brother– threatened him into robbing the bank to steal the letter Nithercott mentioned to prevent further digging into *Deadly Deerstalker*. He took a couple of extras as a decoy, and they didn't take more so as not to have been overburdened with stolen correspondence. As you know, the whole plan backfired. The three letters were burnt, by the way. Graysen says Rupert tore them up, tossed them into a metal bowl, and threw a lit match on top of them."

"The two of them were flatmates, even though they didn't get along?" Zabel wondered.

"Well, they aren't that successful. They don't make much money from their productions, and they inherited the flat from their grandfather. They live and work together out of convenience and business, not because of love and loyalty. My time's up. No more questions."

Zabel tried to coax more information out of the Inspector, but he had clearly had more than his recommended daily allotment of us, and he was out the door with nothing more than the briefest possible "goodbye."

The four of us looked at each other after the Inspector's departure for a few moments. After inhaling the last dangling noodle, Jasper looked at us expectantly. "Is there any ice cream for dessert?" he asked. When I answered in the affirmative, he took a big bowl of chocolate ice cream with him into his room so he could join a YouTube chat on recent revivals of 1980s animated series with some of his closest online friends that he'd never met in real life.

There isn't much left to say. Not too long afterwards, Rupert Fortescue pled guilty to manslaughter and the charges connected to the bank robbery, and confirmed pretty much everything the Inspector told us. His half-brother Graysen remained a free man, having received little more than a finger wag and a "naughty, naughty, naughty" from the judge. Graysen went on to shift Mute Swans' focus, and started producing "social justice-conscious programming." His next two television movies received glowing reviews from critics. About a hundred people total actually watched them. Their father passed away a few months later in a small hotel in Japan, and his side of the story was never shared. The case never got much traction in the media... until Zabel and I started telling the story.

This was the case that turned Zabel from a minor independent true crime reporter to a full-fledged star. Her videos on this narrative went viral, and when an enterprising literary agent suggested turning our adventures into a book, Zabel pointed out that I was the one with stronger prose skills, so the result of my efforts is this manuscript. Zabel and I started collaborating on numerous mini-documentaries of interesting crimes, and the results have been fun and moderately profitable.

I'm still working at the bank, as the work is easy and fun and it gives me plenty of time to work on my own writing. Thanks to my new notoriety, I've even gotten a rather nice raise. I have been receiving three times as much mail lately, though much of this new mail is addressed specifically to me, by fans of Zabel's videos and podcasts, asking questions about our investigations and occasionally even asking for my help with various problems.

One letter in particular caught my eye:

Dear Mr. Zhuang,

Hello! I'm writing to you from Inverness, Scotland. As a fan of Sherlock Holmes, you are no doubt familiar with the Inverness Cape, and also how the most famous body of water in the general vicinity, Loch Ness, is connected to the 1970 Billy Wilder movie "The Private Life of Sherlock Holmes." Assuming you've seen that movie, you know that a critical plot point focuses on the Loch Ness Monster and a government secret. When Wilder was filming the movie, he made a change to the design of the Loch Ness Monster prop, which led to it sinking to the bottom of the Loch. The long-lost prop was recently rediscovered several years ago, but for a while now, some people have tried to have the "head" of the "Loch Ness Monster" raised from the bottom of the deep. Last week, a couple of young enthusiasts attempted to retrieve the head, but they both disappeared mysteriously. We're not sure what happened to them, but we don't believe that they drowned, as no empty boat was found on the water, and all of their diving equipment was left in their hotel room. The local authorities have found some notes in their room connected to the film "The Private Life of Sherlock Holmes," but their journals have a ton of references that only a Sherlock Holmes expert would be able to understand. As a fan of Miss Carvalho's videos, I thought of you, and I hope that you can come here to help us with our questions, please. Thank you!

> *Sincerely,*
> *Senior Constable Pherson Waldroup*

Soon afterwards, Zabel and I took a trip up to Loch Ness to investigate this case. It proved to be a far more interesting and dangerous adventure that we initially anticipated, and when we got into serious trouble, Sanna and Jasper (who left the flat for the first time in years) were compelled to come to Scotland to rescue us and help us find out who was behind the disappearances.

But that's another story.

Also from Chris Chan

To Sherlock Holmes, Irene Adler is "the woman." In "A Scandal in Bohemia," she defeated him in his attempt to retrieve an incriminating photograph of the King of Bohemia. Or did she? In the tradition of "The Great Game," this book will explore the unanswered questions in "A Scandal in Bohemia," illustrating that there is much more to the case than is generally suspected. Why did Holmes make so many elementary mistakes? Was Holmes really a cocaine user? Was the King of Bohemia hiding a dark secret? Why was the photograph so dangerous? Why was Irene Adler in such a hurry to get married? Was Irene Adler really a blackmailer? These and more questions will be answered by studying the clues and contradictions in the original story, which lead to a shocking conclusion.

About MX Publishing

MX Publishing is the world's largest specialist Sherlock Holmes publisher, with over four hundred titles and two hundred authors creating the latest in Sherlock Holmes fiction and non-fiction.

Our largest project is The MX Book of New Sherlock Holmes which is the world's largest collection of new Sherlock Holmes Stories – with over two hundred contributors including NY Times bestsellers Lee Child, Nicholas Meyer, Lindsay Faye and Kareem Abdul-Jabbar. The collection has raised over $85,000 for Stepping Stones School for children with learning disabilities.

Learn more at www.mxpublishing.com

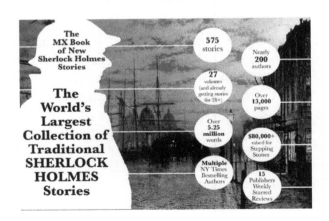

(as of May 2021 – more volumes on the way!)

218

Lightning Source UK Ltd.
Milton Keynes UK
UKHW010100171121
394082UK00002B/584